Queer & Loathing IN WONDERLAND

(POLLUTO #4)

This special edition is limited to 100 hardback deluxe copies and 500 paperback copies. Released Winter 2009 by Dog Horn Publishing.

This is copy ___ of ___.

Signed _____

Adam Lowe, Editor-in-Chief

CONTENTS

Contributor biographies and editor's letter available at Polluto.com. Read 'Queer & Loathing on the Yellow Brick Road' and take part in the competition online. Prize: one year's free subscription.

Polluto is published four times a year by Dog Horn Publishing at £7.99 for the limited edition paperback and £24.99 for the deluxe hardback. Subscriptions are £30 per year in the UK. Please check polluto.com for international rates and stockists.

Editor-in-Chief: Adam Lowe
Creative Director: Michael Dark
Acquisitions Editors: John Diviney, Victoria Hooper
Artist-in-Residence: Dave Migman
Columnists: RC Edrington, Micci Oaten
Front Cover Art: Ignacio Candel
Back Cover Art: Luke Drozd
Interior Art: Elaine Borthwick, Luke Drozd, Dave Migman, Flavia Testa-Lytle

To stock *Polluto* or any other Dog Horn title, please email sales@doghornpublishing.com.

Dog Horn Publishing
6 Athlone Terrace, Armley, Leeds LS12 1UA
UNITED KINGDOM

Alice In The Palace

by
Dave Migman

Christ this fucken little dress doesn't fit. I'm too big. I'm growing. Goddamned pills. Bursting out and where's that rabbit? Sure I saw a fucken rabbit . . . poxy little bastard! Where are you?

Someone gave me a pill. I was at this weird house fulla freaks. I'm straight. I pride myself on that. I thought it was E. What the fuck is this? Place? Space?

I'm coming up . . . Again! Christ. How did I get into this little dress? Blue and white checks. I'm like a giant teddy bear stuffed into a dolls dress.

In the mirror I am a giant . . . Bear . . . bare . . . someone draped across me. The Queen of Tarts is on her knees. Flat as a pancake. Stuffing my cock into her gummy mouth. The King crawls up behind me and rams something in. In. IN!

Where's my dress? I want my dress. Something wet dribbling between my legs. Someone said, I just fucked Alice right up the arse!

I'm not Alice. I'm Derek. I work in the bank. Jim invited me here. Little Jim the cashier. You like to party? Oh yes. Oh, then you'll really like my party.

Spiked me . . . didn't someone just . . . rape me? I'm shrinking. There are shelves all around me. Bottles full of lizards and rolling eyes. Everyone shrinking together. Swallowed into the king's royal gullet. A giant mouth kissing my belly, sucking my cock, sticking a tongue up my arsehole.

Shrinking . . . sucked . . . sucking . . . fucking . . . fucker.

Where'd the rabbit go? I saw it. I chased it through the crowd. Rancid little bastard. It had some kind of disease. It was covered with orange pustules. But god, it looked me in the eye and I knew right then how she felt. Alice. Right through the fucking looking glass. It was like it had a lot to say. It held answers and I ran through the house. The crowd moved thick around me; like slime they stuck to me; my clothes were pulled free and I could no longer breathe. When finally I broke free there I was, in that little dress (where'd it go?) and in the palace. No longer the party.

What is this? What is going on? Must be a dream. Hallucination. But the Queen appears and takes my hand. Feels real. She is a card! Naked. Her tits hang thing and long. They dangle like useless udders and get tangled around her knees. She tumbles and points towards the garden. I go. I want to find my little dress.

I WANT MY FUCKEN DRESS!

A bridge of bodies, naked and locked together in heavenly coitus. I squirm across. Hands stoke me, pull me, poke me, prod and abuse me. Tongues flicker, orifices are flowers gaping wanton and petals of skin invite pollin-ation.

I'm exhausted by the time I reach the other side. I'm spent, shrivelled. A husk. I need to inflate into that little fucken dress.

I need to be Alice.

I'm ALICE!

Hallo. Welcome. Says the tiny man with the oversized head. Come on, Alice. Welcome back. You know it's time, Alice. He has a terrible glint in his eyes. I know he wants to do something to me. Something he has done to little Alice before. Time and time again.

Yes . . . yes.

He smiles. His teeth are tiny points. The not-so-white rabbit approaches. I have answers it seems to be saying as it smiles and hands the swollen headed hatter a cleaver.

Time. They all call in unison.

Time I say.

The End

The Parasol Clerks

by
Rhys Hughes

"Laugh if you will . . . They laughed at all great ideas and inventions. They laughed at nitrous oxide."

JOHN SLADEK

At the end of a hectic morning, Theo found himself sitting in a waiting room and trying to catch the eye of the receptionist, a pretty blonde girl called Claire, not because he thought he stood a chance with her in a sexual or romantic sense but in order to ask for her advice. She resolutely ignored him and he was unable to bring himself to interrupt her with his question, so he continued to sit there until a door opened and he was summoned by a voice.

"We're ready to see you now."

He stood and passed through the door into another room which contained two chairs. He exchanged nods with a woman with an intense gaze and accepted her invitation to sit opposite her. Her name was Fran. The room was so small it was impossible for him to adjust his position without touching her, so he kept his legs and feet immobile and found this hampered his ability to talk persuasively. He was aware he sounded feeble and unconfident.

"If you don't mind, I'd like to ask a question."

"With respect, Mr Geller, that normally happens at the end of the interview. First I should explain the function of our organisation and outline your duties in the event you are ultimately accepted for the post."

"But that's just it, I don't actually want a job here."

Fran chuckled politely at what she assumed was a joke. "It's not really a job, more of a placement. There are no wages as such, though you'll be paid a small living allowance and the experience itself is invaluable. Surely you must concede it's preferable to being unemployed?"

"I don't doubt that, but I already have a job."

"Yes, but you *look* unemployed and that's enough, I've double checked the rules. Consider the shabbiness of your clothes, the disorder of your hair and pungency of your odour. You might as well be unemployed and to all intents and purposes that's what you are. It's a matter of perspective."

"But does that justify kidnapping me?"

Fran blinked alarmingly. "How else would we recruit enough staff? Our operation is vital to society. I'm suppose I might be willing to bend the rules just once and let you ask your question. What is it?"

He raised his arms and indicated his bonds.

"Will you please cut me loose?"

Π

He was led to the top floor of the building to meet his supervisor, who was engaged in playing a game on his computer. Theo saw penguins or something equally small and cute, lots of them, hopping across a landscape that was desolate, evocative and easy for a programmer to create. The supervisor glanced sideways at the new arrival and mumbled a reasonable greeting.

"My name is Andi and I've been here for seven years. You can have the desk in the corner and maybe time will tell."

Theo frowned. "Tell what?"

"Whether I notice or forget you. Just don't hope for promotion, the big bosses like to move staff members *laterally* because it saves money and distributes the wear on the carpets. Why do you want to work here?"

Theo sniffed. "I wasn't given a choice."

"Room for improvement on your motivation but not a bad start, I like the way you perch on the edge of your chair."

"I'm a little apprehensive, I guess."

"Keep it like that, it looks good, as if you're alert—I sometimes feel I'm the only person in the building who isn't slumbering or trying to escape or attempting suicide. Or am I the only worker who *is* doing those things? I keep getting it mixed up but I'm basically satisfied with my lot."

"Are you? Why is that?"

Andi winked slyly. "A lot is better than too much."

Theo glanced around and noticed a squat woman sitting rigidly at a desk near the window. Her blank eyes were magnified into polluted lagoons by the thick lenses of unfashionable spectacles and her jowls hung low in various shades of grey. An odour of pickled putrescence lingered about her.

"Is she daydreaming?" he enquired.

"Who knows? An alternative hypothesis is that she's dead. It's hard to say because she never goes completely off, just drifts in and out of decay. The current rumour is that she's allergic to the entire universe and so avoids *everything*, including motion, breathing, sentience—even death!"

Theo scratched his head. "She can't be much fun to work with."

"We call her the Milky Bar Corpse."

Theo lowered his voice. "Whatever for?"

"No whispering! She's allergic to that as well. You'll bring her out in a giant rash and the office is cluttered enough as it is. Too late! It's like a postcard sunset in here now. That's a point against you, young fellow."

Π

Induction Lecture:

What are we? Why, how and when?

SCVS is an umbrella organisation dedicated to taking over, adapting and improving many of the so called 'services' that were formerly offered by local government. We were set up for the sake of regional and general humanity but both types of humanity have so far proved disappointingly ungrateful. No matter, we can live with that. We have partner organisations in many other cities working to similar aims but the evidence remains that we are the biggest, most efficient and smartest of them all. For the past decade we have been overachieving, outperforming and upstaging. We do it well and our cellars are extensive.

Although we prefer to make all the first moves, voluntary groups and individuals (members of the public—known as MOPS) may utilise our services, establishing contact with us by telephone or *other means* and arranging meetings in a variety of rooms. We may even give them what they want—support, money, the cold honest truth. A dirty but necessary job.

Despite convincing evidence to the contrary, Swansea is a graceful city of charm and culture, a damn good place to live and work, but local government keeps letting it down. Bad local government!

Remember this statement—we are an umbrella organisation.

Umbrella. What does that mean to you?

Think about it. A single unit stretching over smaller elements. Not a web, grid or matrix. Not a saucepan filled with many different and often contradictory ingredients blended into a single complex taste. Not even a mushroom. An umbrella. Write that word down and keep it safe. Umbrella. Without holes.

We want you here. We need you.

The work is not without its hazards. Staff may feel threatened or intimidated by disgruntled outsiders who call in for advice. The directors are planning to fit a panic button to protect our employees.

We hope you will be safe and take good care.

Enjoy your working life with us. Please.

One last word of advice—never fuck with Amanda.

Π

"There's a lot of banging going on somewhere," said Theo, inclining his head to one side. "Do you have the workmen in?"

Andi nodded. "Far below in the deepest basement, no real idea what they're doing down there—I don't know either."

"In that case how do you know they don't know?"

"Because I've been a *working man* for seven years, not *unemployed* like certain individuals. You're interrupting my game, by the way."

"What's the score?" asked Theo.

"Difficult to say, I tend to play fifty or sixty at the same time and it's hard keeping track of what's going on but I can reveal that one of my games involves manipulating people according to specific rules, real people, the people who toil and struggle in this building right here. I'm a Grandmaster of Lives. Which reminds me: it's your turn to make the coffee, eight sugars please."

Π

Loose talk in the kitchen at lunchtime. Loosely rolled cigarettes and the gurglings of the water dispenser, wobbly plastic cups crunched underfoot and the harsh music of spoons rattling against coffee jars.

On the side nearest the door . . .

"I'm learning the language of the orcs."

"Really Gareth? I went to Orkney for my holidays years ago but I didn't pick up any of the local tongue. It's funny because the previous year I went to Brighton and had lots of it thrust down my throat."

"I can say *one large beer please* in orc-ish."

"How would you say it in English?"

Gareth pondered carefully. "*Gizza-fckingpint*, I think."

"Rather an ugly language, isn't it?"

"Yes but old and mysterious and popular."

Agnes stormed into the room. "Who put the Milky Bar Corpse in the freezer again? It spoils the fishcakes. No jamming her in the ventilation shaft either, that's even worse for our health. And no applying for her job under my nose, *the paperwork is deeply unpleasant and the vaccines agonising*."

Π

"I couldn't find the kitchen," blushed Theo.

"What do you mean? It's downstairs, first right, through the Cretan Labyrinth and halfway into the Vale of Nepenthe."

"I must have taken a wrong turning. I ended up on the roof instead, there's a sort of observatory there, huge telescope."

"How do you know it's not a microscope used by aliens to study us?"

Theo was flustered. "I can't say."

Andi glowered. "Well you should, you're a professional now and you work for SCVS, if you don't take responsibility for things like that the local government will claim them back and that's bad news for all."

"It's a radio telescope with a big dish, no lenses at all, so maybe that's why it can't be a microscope. I guess that's my answer."

Andi sighed. "Not quick enough, but nice try."

A girl entered the office and threaded her way between the desks.

"Has anybody seen my mobile phone?"

"When did you last see it?" Andi demanded.

"It's in my pocket right now but I know I'm bound to lose it soon, so I'm preparing myself to find it early by tracking it beforehand."

Theo responded petulantly, "I haven't seen it and I can't guess where it is. I don't seem to know anything. I don't even know what SCVS *stands for*. I still can't work it out and it's making me very nervous."

Andi overheard him. "Acronymophobia . . . Incurable . . . "

Π

Theo was still learning the ropes.

He tugged the one which dangled above his head. A pulley turned slowly and a handbook for new employees rose from its lost position behind a rusty filing cabinet. By pulling on a second rope he was able to swing it over his desk and drop it before him. Cobwebs creaked as he turned the pages and his eyes felt like the feet of flies as they ran across the rotten words.

"The big bosses of SCVS are three in number and rule together—you may call them the Carol Junta, or maybe there are not three but a single one seen in three different contexts, to wit:

•Green Carol

•Amber Carol

•Red Carol

"The one you meet first will possibly determine how good you feel about yourself for the rest of your life. Do not jump a Red Carol and resist the temptation to gamble with an Amber Carol. Apart from that you are free within set limits. Do not ask what those limits are, our patience is limited.

"Even infinite things can have parameters."

Theo nodded at these wise words but failed to understand them.

Π

Kim and Jan were rearranging box files in the archives, another name for searching for odd objects hidden away by funny people. Jan had already secured a bottle of whisky and a lump of quality hashish. Kim had found a thigh bone charred at both ends and riddled with teeth marks.

"It must have been a very funny person who left this here."

"Everybody has funny things about them."

"Tell me some of the funny traits of our colleagues."

"Well the funny thing about Sarita is that she's always losing things, she'd forget her own head if it had any memories in it which could be lost, but they've all gone long ago. I guess she's safe in that respect."

"I wish I was safe," sighed Kim.

"In what way aren't you?"

"I started an archery class yesterday and thought it might be a good idea to use my nipple ring as a rest for the arrow—to keep it straight while I aimed. Plus I wanted to experiment with the tickle of the feather after the shot has been fired. So I notched the arrow, took a meditative breath and let it fly."

"What happened? Did it tug the ring out?"

"No. It hit the centre of the target. My instructor concluded that I was so good at archery it was time for an evolutionary step in my leisure pursuits. He wants me to start using a musket instead, an old fashioned flintlock. I'll need a bigger nipple ring and I'm worried about the recoil on my aureole. Like I said I don't feel safe now. No matter. Tell me another funny trait."

"That new worker who has just started with us—Theo Geller—he doesn't know that SCVS stands for Swansea Council *for* Voluntary Service. He can't even work that out. What a buffoon."

"Those are just the sort of workers we probably need."

"Yes. Look inside this file. Broad beans!"

II

The latest word on the street is the same as what it was before, don't ever fuck with Amanda, don't think about trying it on with her, not now, not any time, she's not in the mood for it and that's a key word you need to remember if you want to survive your encounter with her. Mood. That's the word on the street but which street? Fifth Avenue, Tobacco Road, the Camino del Rey? None of those, I'm talking about the metaphorical street of wisdom, the street where pedestrians keep their teeth intact and balls unbruised, if you know what I'm saying, and you do know what I'm saying, don't you? Sure you do. Keep safe.

(SCVS Press Release)

II

Some staff members with descriptive traits:

Amanda . . . . . . Conditioner of MOPS and Press Release Writer,

Mistress Mel . . . . . . Her tastes run to the unusual and painful,

Fran . . . . . . The Gazer, the Looker, the Intimidator,

The Flaxen Midget . . . . . . Not the brightest spark in the dying bonfire,

Julia . . . . . . Feathery earrings and stripes on socks,

David . . . . . . One iron hand, one of wood, his brain exists in the 5th Century,

Gail . . . . . . Smokes too much, likes flicking beans,

Allyson . . . . . . Still believes that computers run on punched cards,

Mike . . . . . . Financial genius, other qualities unknown,

Oscar . . . . . . His assistant and catamite,

Horace . . . . . . A fig tree without extensive duties,

Claire . . . . . . A receptionist, keeper of the Portal to Misery,

Gareth . . . . . . Believes in the planet Vulcan,

Adrian . . . . . . Has to be first in every list (please read from bottom up).

Π

"Hello, has anybody seen my ruler?

"What's happened to my pencil?

"I seem to have misplaced my handbag again.

"Anybody seen my trousers?

"Where's that pesky punctuation mark?

"My chair? My desk?

"My office, city, nation? Where are they? How do I make a reverse charge call from here? What's the code from Ouarzazate?

"Hello . . . hello . . . terrible line. Sandstorm.

"Yes I know where my mobile phone is . . .

"But I've lost my pocket . . . "

Π

"Do you know anything about the Drake equation?"

"The one which states that the number of advanced technical civilisations in our galaxy is equal to the number of stars in the galaxy multiplied by the fraction of stars that have planetary systems multiplied by the number of Earth-like planets in these systems multiplied by the fraction of suitable planets on which life actually arises multiplied by the fraction of inhabited planets on which intelligent life evolves multiplied by the fraction of planets inhabited by intelligent beings that attempt to communicate multiplied by the frac-

tion of the planet's life for which the civilisation survives?"

"Yes, that one."

"No, afraid I don't. Sorry."

"But do you think it has anything to do with the observatory on the roof? Do you think that someone in SCVS in engaged in a search for extraterrestrial intelligence? Maybe the organisation is a front?"

"Claire seems to know more about it than anyone else. Why not ask her?"

"She's on her lunch break. Shall I ask the Milky Bar Corpse? I know that's taking a pointless risk—because she's bound not to know—but it might show that we are trying to engage her, make her feel part of a team. Besides, there's hope even for her, isn't there? Miracles can happen logically. One day she might develop an allergy to allergic reactions and get better."

"Or worse, depending on the strength of the paradox."

"You're right, I'm an idealist."

Π

How did it happen, this manifestation in his office? Not that it wasn't welcome as a change from the usual routine, he didn't intend to complain or even file a report, but all the same he had enough work to do and now it would be an ordeal just to reach his desk. He wasn't dressed for this environment.

Adrian closed the door again and stood quietly in the corridor for a minute before taking another look. No, he wasn't dreaming, his office really had turned into a jungle, a very small jungle, or rather there was a jungle inside his office. The day before and innumerable other days previous to that there had only been papers and machinery and cabinets and his colleagues.

He stepped over the threshold and the heat hit him, a humid stickiness that drained all his energy and made his skin prickle under his suit. He removed his jacket and used it to shield his face from thorns and vines coated in sap which dangled from the ceiling. The noise of parrots was astounding. To his left bubbled a quicksand and beyond that an enormous stinking flower nodded its meaty petals at his passing. He pinched his nostrils with his free hand.

At irregular intervals he called the names of his fellow workers.

They didn't reply. He pushed on.

Adrian worked at the far end of the office and his normal procedure was to simply walk in a straight line from door to desk, but today this proved to be an impossible task. His new route took him over tangled roots, under half fallen trees and along the circumference of a miniature lagoon. Eventually he reached his customary place and discovered that his chair and desk were still there.

Not knowing what else to do, he sat and opened the window. The roar and bustle of the city slapped him in the face. He leaned out and looked down onto the street at the hurrying crowds and crawling traffic. Then he looked out over the rooftops at the dirty factory chimneys in the distance.

Closing the window, he started work in a cloud of insects. An unseen monkey dropped nuts on his head from above.

Π

MEMO TO ALL STAFF MEMBERS:

THIS IS A LIST OF OUTSTANDING MEMOS:

Memo: Adrian must always be associated with this position in every list,

Memo: No private phone calls to paramours and blackguards,

Memo: Sarita has lost her keys again,

Memo: The Milky Bar Corpse must not be stored,

Memo: Play one (old) joke on Agnes,

Memo: Sarita has lost her pink/orange/red folder,

Memo: Sarita has lost this memo,

Memo: MEMO TO ALL STAFF MEMBERS:

THIS IS A LIST OF OUTSTANDING MEMOS:

Memo: Adrian must always be associated with this position in every list,

Memo: No private phone calls to paramours and blackguards,

Memo: Sarita has lost her keys again,

Memo: The Milky Bar Corpse must not be stored,

Memo: Play one (old) joke on Agnes,

Memo: Sarita has lost her pink/orange/red folder,

Memo: Sarita has lost this memo,

Memo: MEMO TO ALL STAFF MEMBERS:

THIS IS A LIST OF OUTSTANDING MEMOS:

Memo: Adrian must never be associated with this position in every list,

Memo: No private phone calls to paramours and blackguards,

Memo: Sarita has lost her keys again,

Memo: The Milky Bar Corpse must not be stored,

Memo: Play one (old) joke on Agnes,

Memo: Sarita has lost her pink/orange/red folder,

Memo: Sarita has lost this memo,

Memo: Parallel universes do exist and they may be almost exactly like our own universe with one or two trivial deviations.

Π

"They've installed a panic button downstairs," said Fran.

Mike looked up from his ledger. "It's a good idea. Just in case members of the public get trapped in a corner with Amanda. It's not actually wired to anything, it's a placebo to ease their final moments."

"Where is Amanda now anyway?"

Mike glanced over his shoulder. "Killing sperm with a mallet."

Fran snorted. "About time somebody did it, I nearly slipped and bashed my skull yesterday on the toilet bowl. Why can't boys wait for lunchbreaks and pop home for a quick one like the girls? Sheer laziness."

Π

"I've got bad news. Our AM coffee break has been cancelled."

"Don't be absurd. How can any worker function without an AM coffee break? We've always had an AM coffee break."

"No longer it seems. From tomorrow it's finished."

"Where did you hear this rumour?"

"From Green Carol herself. No disputing her orders."

"How are we supposed to cope?"

"We're going to get an FM coffee break instead."

"What exactly is the difference?"

"When we walk to the kitchen to make coffee—and when we return with the coffee itself—we're not allowed to bob up and down with a variable amplitude. The peak and trough of every bob must be identical. However, we are allowed, indeed *required*, to vary the length of each step."

"I supposed we'll get used to it."

"Yes and the reception for our coffee will be better."

"Good. The last time I made coffee for my office they all scowled."

Π

Andi was discussing his own death.

"Some people leave their bodies to medical science but I plan to leave mine to a necrophiliac – just so that I know I'm having one last fling even when I'm gone. It might catch on."

Theo was dubious. "I'd want to be able to choose who was going to have my corpse before I died."

"Why does that matter? You won't know about it."

"I don't want some fat guy who bites my shoulder and keeps losing his balance and slides off onto the slab. That's undignified. I insist on having a young girl with a removable dildo, otherwise I'm not doing it, I'll get myself cremated instead and deny anybody the pleasure."

"That's a little bit selfish," observed Andi.

Theo shrugged. "Why should the living person be the active partner in necrophilia anyway? Who invented that rule? I don't particularly enjoy being the submissive one, I have such little responsibility in life that I don't need to surrender any in death."

"It's not a rule as such, it's a practicality."

"I don't see why. Maybe I could arrange for my corpse to be wired up to a generator. A flick of a switch and a few thousand volts in my muscles making them flex and twitch. Imagine that. Could be even better than the living thing, come to think about it."

Andi was bitter. "I never expected you to be a pervert. It's something of a disappointment, I must confess."

"May I see your donor card?" Theo asked.

Π

Catarina tiptoed down the corridor and unlocked the stationary cupboard. It was called the stationary cupboard because unlike every other cupboard in the building it didn't move around on its own but stayed in the same location, a valuable reference point on the confusing middle floor. She dragged her diving equipment behind her. She changed quickly and quietly, checked the valves on her tanks and plunged in. A single drop of water splashed the plastic floor.

At once she was immersed in a different world, a flooded grotto through which sunlight from an unknown source wavered and pulsed. Kicking her flippers she dove down towards a reef, bending her body around the crimson forests of coral, between the shoals of bright fish with elaborate fins and shimmering scales. They did not flee. This was her special place, her escape from office drudgery, a secret known only to her, and the denizens of this misplaced deep were familiar with her and accepted her presence as a natural part of the environment.

Every lunchtime she attempted to explore the limits of this inner sea, constantly amazed that it seemed to stretch on forever. A spare hour simply wasn't long enough for her to determine how large it was. She contented herself with just existing among the wonders, relishing the exotic sights, the freedom, the release from tedium. It was hers alone, a private cosmos of wonder.

But today something was wrong. An uneasy feeling.

She kept going down, frowning behind her mask, trying to ignore the itch on her nose which confirmed that trouble lay ahead.

On the seabed an octopus waved at her. It clutched objects in each of its tentacles. It seemed distressed or perhaps victorious, it was difficult to tell with such creatures. The owners of suckers had incomprehensible values, she had learned that from long experience. They were rubbery in motives as well as appendages. A cloud of black ink drifted slowly around her.

She approached the octopus and squinted at the objects.

A chill ran up her spine, panic gripped her heart. The ink had not come from the creature but from what it held. Books. Works of fantasy and science fiction. Grimly she smiled to herself, for her knowledge of Spanish had suggested a pun to her. Pulp fiction, *pulpo*. It was no consolation.

The octopus held up the volumes for her inspection.

The titles on gaudy covers were still legible. *Beyond the Twisted Fangs*, *Lord of the Big Sword*, *Black God's Snog*, *Agents of the Molten Hammer*, *Mighty Thews*, *Eggs of the Dragon*, *Pasta of the Gorgon*, *Chips of the Hippogriff*. These last three clearly constituted an unhealthy trilogy.

She turned away aghast. Her secret was out.

Somehow Gareth had discovered how to open the cupboard!

Π

"I found this sign," said Theo.

"Where did you find it?" asked Andi.

"In a pocket lying around on the floor. It wasn't connected to anything and my foot kicked it before I looked down."

"There are signs everywhere in this building, some are bound to get misplaced on occasions. What does it say? Show me."

Theo passed it to him:

THE MILKY BAR CORPSE
IS ALLERGIC TO THIS SIGN!

(keep her away)

"What shall I do with it?" he asked.

Andi consulted his book of obscure rules. "Take it to the Person Responsible for Handling Lost Signs. That's the procedure."

"Who might that be?" Theo scratched his head.

"The Milky Bar Corpse. She's so useless at important work that we gave her a simple duty to make her feel included."

"That was very rash." Theo was learning quickly.

"Yes, I know, don't remind me."

Theo remembered something. "That wasn't the only sign I found, I found another, more a diagram than a sign, a Venn diagram."

Andi took this as well and studied it.

"I can't work out its meaning," confessed Theo.

Andi licked his suddenly dry lips. "It's not a Venn diagram or a schematic of any sort. *It's a portrait drawn from life!*"

Π

Green Carol called Theo in for a meeting. Fran lurked in the background performing an eye test on a chart pinned to the far wall.

"We've made a mistake. An error in the paperwork, you should never have been forced into a placement with us."

Theo sighed with relief. "I'm glad you've worked that out."

"Using modern methods of nomenclature analysis, I can specify what individuals should *really* be. It's all very logical.

"Your full name is Theodore Travis Geller, correct?

"Well look closely at this:

Theodore Travis Geller
Theo Trav Eller
The Trav eller
The Traveller

"By removing certain letters I can determine your real calling. You are a traveller and should be on a beach in Brazil or Thailand dancing to trance music. This meth-od never fails. Last year a new recruit was pressganged into SCVS and he rose rapidly to become a director. I knew this outcome was inevitable and recommended him for promotion on the basis of my insight.

"His given name was:

Jonas Slick Ericson

"I think you may leave now, Mr Geller, I've explained myself adequately. It's too late to let you back out into the world, I'm afraid, so you'll just have to carry on with shards of bitterness in your soul."

Fran turned to them in delight. "My intensity is still perfect."

Theo left quietly. Back in his own office, he asked Andi, "What exactly do we do here? I still don't know. *What do we do?*"

From somewhere unseen The Flaxen Midget gurgled.

Andi acted as interpreter, "We're administrators—no justification is required for that, we are beyond explanation."

The Flaxen Midget babbled something else.

Theo cast a look of expectancy at Andi, who responded with a shrug. "She's just worked out that she can work things out."

"That's amazing. Isn't it?"

"Shh! She's trying to say something else. Three statements in a row!"

"What was this latest one?" cried Theo.

"She's just worked out—using her new ability at working things out—that there are three spatial dimensions, not two."

"That's a big step," commiserated Theo.

"You're talking about *length*, the dimension which has escaped her attention until now is *depth*. So it's not a step, more of a jump. As for height being a mystery to her, it's one of the hazards of being a Flaxen Midget. How could she have noticed before? It was outside not only her parameters of experience but the very format of her being. Plus she's an imbecile."

"That makes it harder," agreed Theo.

Π

In the kitchen near the locked emergency exit . . .

"My office has become a jungle," said Adrian.

"That's what modern life is all about," sighed Catarina.

"No a *literal* jungle. With creepers. Not that this is unusual for me. Years ago I had an office with a lost civilisation in it, a stranded galleon overgrown with orchids, and monks who knew the secret of eternal youth but they wouldn't tell me what it was, not that it mattered because I already knew it. I also had offices which were literal deserts, atolls and nightclubs."

"You really have done everything first, haven't you?"

"Yes and I was the very first person to do everything first. All other firsts came after my firsts, at best they are second or even third *firsts*. My firsts are both a boon and a curse in a variety of ways but they don't interfere with my role in this organisation. That's a first too."

"You didn't get a first in your degree though . . . "

"No, I did better than that. I got a half. I was the first person to get a half, they would have given me a minus number but problems can arise if you try to square root *those* so I gladly accepted the smallest positive number they were willing to quote. I was the first person not to get an integer as a rating for my graduation, I also used to play in a post punk band."

Catarina smirked. "What were they called?"

"*The Unsigned Twats* . . . Post punk and anti ironic—in fact we were *ironiclasts* dedicated to purging the world of posts and replacing them with protos. Everything we ever did was not normally new."

"You mean it was old?" frowned Catarina.

"No it was *abnormally* new. We caused a stir locally, people would recognise us in the street. 'Twats!' they would call."

"Maybe they were being ironic?" suggested Catarina.

"Oh no, they really meant it!"

Π

"Don't those workmen ever stop for a single moment? Banging away day after day, night after night, from dawn to dusk and between nocturne and aubade, all the time without surcease or even sandwiches."

"I know what you mean. You've joined a poetry circle."

"By what token did you fathom that, O charming soul?"

"Don't know . . . A hunch . . . But you're right about those workmen. Something else a bit funny—I went back to the archives and dug around in a few more box files and I found the architect's plans for this building. The cellars are bigger than I imagined, a hell of a lot bigger. They go on and on for nearly the length of the entire street. With the aid of my abracadabracus I've worked out there's more spare cubic metres below ground than above. SCVS is an iceberg."

"Yes they never show their bulk, do they? Chill scallywags!"

Elsewhere in the office commotion reigned . . .

Allyson was in tears. "My computer has broken again!"

"No it hasn't," said Jan, "you just haven't plugged it in, I can see the plug dangling loose. There's no power reaching it."

"No *my* computer, the one I use every day."

"Which one is that?"

"In the kitchen. It doesn't work anymore. There's a little person trapped inside it jamming the flowcharts and other internal components. I don't know how they got in there, it's not fair and it's not right."

"A little person? You mean The Flaxen Midget?"

"Smaller. And distorted."

They went down together for a look.

"See, there it is. Just like I said."

Jan bit her lip. "That's not a computer. It's the water dispenser."

She leaned closer and peered carefully. "And that's not a little person but your own reflection in the liquid."

Allyson dried her eyes. "So why has it stopped working?"

"Full of bus tickets. Somebody has been jamming bus tickets up the spout, used bus tickets—return fares—punched pieces of paper . . . "

She turned a withering look on Allyson. "Sometimes I think we ought to put you out with the Babbage . . . I mean garbage."

Allyson was shocked. "I'm not ready for an upgrade!"

Π

"Listen I'm going to have to hang up now, you're a paramour and for all I know some sort of blackguard into the bargain, and if you still want to go out for dinner just find a restaurant and do it, I sure as hell won't be going with you so you can get that idea out of your head right now. In fact I'm never going to speak to you again and you'll never see me either. Yes I know you've been coming here every single night for weeks and using the observatory on the roof but that's no longer appropriate and I've stopped sleeping under the telescope, I have a house of my own now, and I never noticed when you were around anyway, we just aren't made for each other, so I suggest you go away and leave me alone."

"Claire, I hope you don't mind me pointing this out, but that's not a telephone you're using. It's a ouija board."

"Really? That makes sense. Some guy called Ptolemy. He can't seem to get the message, our conversation keeps going round in circles. By the way, Kim, a parcel arrived for you in the shape of a musket."

"I know, and nipple rings have gone metric. It's not my day."

Π

"Adrian is missing. He's the first member of staff to ever do that successfully. I've always admired his ability to get off the mark instantaneously. But we need him back, his talents are irreplaceable.

"Your mission—find and return him . . . "

Catarina entered his office. It seemed normal enough apart from the view out of the window. Instead of the bustling city street she found herself gazing over a jungle scene. She opened the window and thrust out her head. It was the city street again, traffic and pedestrians and litter rushing past. She closed the window and the jungle returned. She half opened the window and peered slyly through the gap but it was the street again, dust and oil stains in the gutters. She closed it to a crack but the breeze that came through still smelled of the city. Only when the window was tightly shut did the jungle reappear for her.

She began opening and closing the window at high speed to confuse whatever process was in operation. This worked. On the twentieth attempt the jungle remained when the window was open to its fullest extent.

She thrust out her head again and listened. Adrian really was out there.

His voice floated from the depths: "But I don't want to be the *first* outsider to be devoured by the Kukuthkuku cannibal tribe . . .

"I'd much rather be the *last* . . . Any chance of that?

"I didn't think so, but . . . Maybe I can become the *first* person to be the last outsider to be eaten in the manner you suggest?

"Yes I like the recipe too, red wine for stock is a nice touch, the cloves and all the other spices, cinnamon, ginger, cardamom . . . I'm not complaining but I can't promise the end result will be very productive."

Parrots drowned out the remainder of his desperation.

Catarina closed the window and left the office. "Can't find him anywhere. I imagine he's mulling over something."

Π

"Guess what happened this morning? Sarita lost her absentmindedness—she put it down somewhere and when she went back it had gone! She's suddenly become the most efficient of us all! There are dozens of new projects being mooted right now, she's meeting with the directors to discuss them, this could be the most exciting and productive time in the history of our organisation and a phenomenal gift to the world and human civilisation, we might be on the brink of a new era for all, an age of pure enlightenment, peace and hope."

"Has anybody lost their absentmindedness? Please pick it up at Reception if you have. It was handed in this morning."

"Damn. Scrap the start of the enlightened age . . . "

Agnes stormed out of the kitchen.

"I don't know which member of staff has a penchant for old jokes but it's making me angry. I went to get a packet of frozen peas and there it was leering at me with icicles of drool hanging from its lips. The Flaxen Midget! Haven't any of you learned the rules of low temperature preservation? You must never jam one of those in the freezer. *It's not big and it's not clever.*"

Silent pencils ticked off one of the memos.

Gail said, "Broad beans aren't really peas, are they?"

Agnes batted her eyelashes.

"Now that's the sort of confrontational playfulness I like."

Π

Green Carol had called a general gathering. From every room in the building, every nook and cupboard, they came to stand in the shadows before her, under her power, her aura, her proven expertise, trembling and chewing their lips but not wishing they had never been born, for that was too small a wish—indeed they had to wish that nobody had ever been born, nobody and nothing, not even the first amoeba, only then might they be assured that this meeting could never have taken place, that it would be a blessed impossibility, that the ladder of evolution would not have led from the sweet hot seas of the Pre-Cambrian Age to Twenty First Century sourness, slowly, painfully, pointlessly. Only then.

But they were not there to be reprimanded.

Green Carol was in a good mood.

She wanted to tell them something, something important, to give them all an explanation, an explanation they deserved.

She began speaking:

"You are victims of a deception, but at the same time you have all done a good job, one which deserves much merit.

"The observatory on the roof should have given the game away.

"SCVS does not stand for what you think it does.

"That's just a front.

"Let me put it this way:

"SCVS does *not* equal Swansea Council *for* Voluntary Service.

"SCVS *does* equal Shield *against* Comets, Volcanoes, Supernovae.

"Or if you want it in mathematical notation:

SCVS = Swansea Council *for* Voluntary Service.

SCVS = Shield *against* Comets, Volcanoes, Supernovae.

"We are indeed an 'umbrella organisation'—literally. The actual purpose of our existence is to protect this planet against incursions from outer space. By incursions I don't mean alien invasion. No that happened a very long time ago and isn't likely to be repeated. The incursions we are concerned with

are natural disasters. Our purpose is to safeguard humanity, all of it, to ensure that men and women continue to exist beyond the allotted span of our race.

"All creatures are subject to extinctions. We might be the first species to buck the trend. That is the whole point of our work.

"In every city a production line has been set up to manufacture umbrellas, not ordinary umbrellas but enormous parasols, thousands of metres in radius, fabricated from titanium and carbon fibre. These production lines are concealed—to prevent the public panicking prematurely—by being located beneath phoney organisations which pretend to provide local services of a particular kind. This is the reason our cellars are so extensive. They are a secret factory. This is also the reason why there is relentless banging. Umbrellas are being made under our very feet. Imagine that! A plethora of brollies! Godlike accessories.

"The umbrella designed to cover Swansea is due to be erected this evening. You will soon see what a wondrous thing it is, far superior to Blackpool Tower—which can't even keep the rain off! Oh yes.

"Our umbrellas will deflect asteroids and comets back into space, prevent hot ash and pyroclastic flows from volcano bursts (including ejecta from volcanic activity on other worlds and moons) settling on people's heads and even reflect the cosmic rays emitted by exploding stars in nearby portions of our galaxy. There will be no repeat of the Permian extinction, I promise you that!

"Right, the lecture is over. Back to work, the useless work you have been doing for weeks, months, years. Bring it on, Armageddon! We're ready for you."

II

"Everything has somehow changed in the past week, I can't quite put my finger on it. I don't mean working conditions or anything like that, it's the world. I mean, look at the sky, it has a sort of musty quality to it, an old faded essence about it, like an old school classroom, the sort we had in the 1970s, but it's not quite like a classroom, it's too quiet and dusty and muted, sort of hushed or suppressed and it smells of mould and has a grubbiness about it, like the clouds have been replaced by huge thumbprints, and it's far too warm all the time."

"Yes, you're right, I hadn't noticed that before."

"Ever since the gigantic umbrellas started going up over every city it has been like this, I'm sure there must be a connection."

"Maybe. But I'm grateful we no longer have to worry about being smashed to bits or fried by ultra hot gamma rays."

"I'm not complaining. Well I guess I am, I shouldn't even be here, I was picked up off the street and forced to work at my desk, I've probably lost my real job, the job I had before I was abducted. But that's not the point. I just don't feel that existence is as open as it was. I feel confined, or rather that the whole human race, the planet, is confined, sort of misplaced, lost, abandoned."

"It could be because . . . well because of what happens when . . . "

"Don't be coy. What's your theory?"

"The world has become forested with gargantuan umbrellas, it is now an umbrella planet, an umbrella rack if you like. The globe can now be defined by its umbrellas, the umbrellas are in essence what it *is*, from space it must surely appear as if we are nothing else. Umbrellas. Our purpose."

"I still don't follow you . . . "

"Look at it this way, what happens to umbrellas? What is the common fate of all umbrellas, whatever their size? Tell me."

"They get lost. In libraries. Usually behind a radiator."

"They do indeed. Indeed they do."

MEMO TO ALL STAFF MEM-
BERS:

The expedition to climb the pole of the Great Swansea Umbrella leaves at noon precisely. Please ensure that you turn up on time. Bring your existing library cards, one other proof of identity and any overdue books in your possession. The last person to leave the building should turn off the lights and set the self destruct timer to one hour. Thank you for your trouble.

The End

Jeanne

by
Steve Redwood

Jeanne is dying. Her dying is returning my strength to me, so I no longer pretend to the others, but go openly into her bedroom and lie beside her, but not like before. All that was bad between us is gone, devoured as she is being devoured, as she would have devoured me, and she is now just a little girl who is lost and defeated and dying, and only half understands why. I lie beside her and rock her gently, and move the damp hair from her terrified eyes with rough callused fingers, and tell her lies, tell her that everything will be all right, and last night I'm sure she whispered, "I couldn't love you before, you know why I couldn't, but now I think I can. Is it too late?" And I lied— or thought I lied—again, and said of course not, and then she cried, the first time she had been able to cry in her whole life; silent, welling adult tears that trickled under my fingers as I stroked her cheek.

I know Alain will never forgive me for this, for robbing him of a part, just a little part, of his prey.

And I am afraid, yes: but the really wonderful thing is, I don't care. Mary, open the curtains again, and let our children look out, you don't have to hide me from them any more.

Π

*Among the so-called solitary wasps, the females confine themselves in most cases to providing food and a sheltered home for the development of their larvae. The normal pattern is for the wasp to make a nest of some sort. These nests reach their highest development in the elegant undivided nests of the potter-wasps (*Eumenes*), each of which shelters a single larva.*

Π

Jeanne's mother, Suzanne. Sitting outside a coffee-house in a village near Périgueux, in the Dordogne, simple yellow dress over a pale slim body, hair that really *was* the colour of corn, cut short and ovalling her face, large light green eyes that looked up at me as I passed, lips that almost curved into a smile. And I, instead of walking on, as I had intended, stopped to gaze at the avalanche of green hills falling on the village, pretended to wipe sweat off my brow, turned back, and took the table next to hers, and thought that *I* was the hunter.

I'd like to say we made love that same night in the old semi-derelict farmhouse she lived in, but that would be wrong: we did the things that adults do when they are making love, so I thought we were making love. A week later, I left my hotel room and moved in.

Of course, I now realise why Suzanne acted as she did: the duty of a mother is to provide for her young. Even at the time, I don't think I ever *really* believed in the miracle: I was fifty-five, muscle turning to flab, hair already grey and attenuate like smoke from a dying fire. From the beginning I paid for everything. When she told me, within a couple of weeks, that she preferred to sleep alone, I wasn't so very surprised, and neither, I must admit, did I really mind. It was still cheaper and pleasanter than the hotel, I enjoyed doing odd jobs, and I had the company of her twelve-year-old daughter, Jeanne.

The farmhouse had already been partly reformed: rooms had been partitioned off, a bathroom constructed with shower and heating rail, electric oven in the kitchen. Yet these things seemed oddly *extraneous*, like a picnic rug on the grass, like a monkey wearing a suit. The floor remained rough and uneven, the stone walls thick and ageless, it retained the smell of the soil and the country, reminding me of pictures of Mr. Badger's house seen as a child, in and of the earth. And Suzanne and her daughter gave the impression of being, like the house, things of nature, fixed, unchanging.

Jeanne. Wild blonde hair that made you ache to catch it in your fingers, the great, solemn green eyes of her mother, freckles like daisies dotting the fields around the valley, child's lips hinting at a woman's heat. Jeanne. My destroyer. My saviour?

The . . . *games* . . . began almost immediately. At first I took no notice when she somehow turned playful kisses on the cheek into kisses on the lips, or when she came and stood by me as I was sawing wood and flung her arms around my thigh, or buried her head between my legs when I sat on the sofa. After all, I had two daughters of my own.

Suzanne began spending more and more time away. It is easy to see now that I should have left. But the poison was already in me: that is why she was not afraid to go. I made excuses for her to myself. After all, could a man of my age really expect to monopolise a woman like her? At least I had a kind of home again. Though I tried not to, at times I remembered Mary in England, with little Sue and Jenny crying beside her, and the shock and loathing on her face, and the curtain drawn tight as if in shame as I started the car. No, I had nothing to go back to.

I really believed it was I who was making the decision to stay.

Π

Confining itself to a class of victims particular to its own species, the female wasp hunts caterpillars, spiders, and other insects. These are stung so that they are paralysed and packed into the cells of the nest.

Π

"Look," Jeanne would say, lifting up her T-shirt, "look how they're growing, come on, you can touch them, if you want to," and sometimes she would jump on me from behind and wrap her legs round my neck so that her thighs were pressed against my lips. I still tried to pretend to myself it was just playfulness (when she never smiled?) but soon I realised I was taking longer to tie my shoes just with the hope that she *would* ambush me, taking a shower without closing the door, looking up into the trees while she picked apples. And though she would sometimes laugh or giggle, she never really smiled: her laughter was strangely savage, it mocked me, clawed at me, tormented me. Her eyes, big strange eyes like her mother's, always looked straight into mine, never around me or beyond me, as in normal human intercourse, but deep into my own eyes, seeking a way, a path, to the vulnerable interior of my being. As if she *knew*.

And still I said to myself that she acted as she did in search of the affection she never received from her mother, even when she *was* at home, which was now almost never. As for her father, it was as if he had never existed. I had asked Suzanne about him, and she said coldly he had served his purpose, and refused to tell me any more, and when I asked Jeanne, she looked mystified, as if the concept of father had no meaning.

I tried to come to terms with what was happening. I sensed that in some visceral way Suzanne had weakened me, had stripped away my defences to leave me exposed to her daughter. My need to hold Jeanne, to rub my cheek against her tiny breasts, to kiss her hair and feel stray strands tickle my tongue, to follow her game, and then make it just that bit more daring—yes, that was already a sickness, but almost worse was the weakness I began to feel every time I was near her, and a growing apathy with anything that was not her. She was feeding on my desire, and on another thing I did not recognise at the time, and the exhilaration of our games slowly turned into something else, a debilitating fear that crawled around the edges of my mind, always there just beyond the reach of consciousness.

One hot August afternoon I found a pile of old books in a big filthy plastic bag in a corner of what had been the stable. Perhaps the owner had been a teacher or a student, because many were on biology, zoology, botany, and related subjects. One, called *Insect Life*, caught my attention, and I browsed through it, fascinated by the complexity and diversity of the subject, terrified by the pre-programmed cruelty of many of these creatures. It was only that night that it occurred to me that those old books should have been covered in cobwebs. I read the book more carefully.

When I accused Jeanne, she cowered away from me, and said I was crazy, and ran into her room, slamming the door on me. But then I hadn't expected her to admit the truth.

Π

The larva that hatches eats its victims alive, and is thus assured of fresh unspoiled food throughout its life; just enough victims are provided for the completion of its growth. Usually the mother wasp has no contact with her offspring beyond the egg stage.

Π

Monique saved me. Or was it Alain? Alain, who hates me because he knows there is a little part of Jeanne he will never have.

They arrived maybe a month ago. I was lying sick and torpid on the bed, and Jeanne's scream broke through the haze and the pain and the slushy greyness that was now my mind. I stumbled into the sitting room and, like a swimmer looking up at an object on the surface, made out Jeanne cowering in a corner away from the door. I crossed the room, put my arms protectively around her, and after a moment she stopped screaming, and subsided into a breathless sobbing. Only then did I turn and see a woman standing in the open doorway with a young boy beside her.

Monique had come from Rouen to see her cousin Suzanne, and wondered why we hadn't received her letter (we had no phone). She didn't show much surprise when I said I hadn't seen Suzanne for more than a week. She's like me, she said, loves to travel. I wasn't the first, she said, to have been left to look after Jeanne.

They had to stay the night, of course, and the next day I found I was feeling better than I had for many days. When Monique asked if I had any objection to them staying a few days, until her cousin returned, I said of course not, it wasn't my place anyway.

Jeanne started to change immediately. I sometimes seemed to catch her —it can't have been my imagination—staring at Alain (for Monique, like Suzanne, tended to disappear most of the time) with hatred and. . .how can I put it, despair. It was as if she recognised a stronger force, a force as elemental as herself, but fresher, more potent.

She became weaker day by day, rarely leaving her room, except sometimes to creep into the garden. I could feel that her power over me had been broken, and I knew why: she would flinch when Alain walked past, though I never saw any violence between the two. Indeed, by then I knew I never would.

Her force, her vitality, was diminishing, and she was fading into. . . . a little girl. A little girl whose death was now as inevitable as the falling of leaves in autumn. And I, as I became stronger, began to feel something quite different towards her. Like I had felt, at the very beginning, for my own two little ones.

I saw her sitting in the garden once, just before the end, her tiny form hunched over the small pond, her shadow being stripped and sucked away under the water, and I went and put my arm around her—this time with none of that gnawing sexual tension —and, without looking up, she said:

"You must leave. Now. In between. After, it will be too late."

I asked her what she meant, and then she did look up at me, confused, her hair stumbling over her cheeks, and said, "What did I say?", and when I repeated her words, she said nothing, but began to tear off strips of bark from a twig with jerky, scrabbling movements, with a look of such terror on her face . . .

I believe I knew what she meant. I sensed that I had been given a reprieve, that there was one small moment, the moment when Jeanne was being destroyed, that I would be free. I even began a weak, pathetic letter to Mary, but I could not drive away the memory of the scorn and fury in her eyes, and knew that I would never send it.

Π

Cleptoparasites, meaning 'thief-parasites', is the best term to apply to the bees and wasps whose breeding habits resemble those of a cuckoo. Indeed, they are often called cuckoo bees and cuckoo wasps. They lay eggs in the nests of solitary wasps and bees, and their larvae feed on those of the host species and on the store of food that has already been collected.

Π

My Jeanne is dead. I watched the life force being sucked out of her, I saw it creeping through every pore, like early morning fog rising out of the Dordogne valleys. At the end, we were united, I and this little pale creature who had been trapped between two worlds, and she must have sensed my tears because I think she whispered, "It wasn't too late, was it?"

Maybe what followed was the rictus of death; I prefer to think it was a smile.

I could have left, before, while Alain was busy with her. I like to think she fought harder to give me that chance, and who is to say it was not so? Is there not sometimes more truth in what might have happened than in what did happen? For a time I had the strength to leave that house that had become too much a part of nature, and I didn't go, because she needed me—or I felt she needed me—or I needed her to need me—and at last I had the chance to expiate so many sins, done and undone.

I had found—no, I really believe I had been *vouchsafed*—the strength to do something greater than escape. *Let thy will be done. . .* The will not to leave her alone with her destroyers, and, by sharing her suffering, the power to wash away the stain and ugliness of everything that had gone before. Yes, she died, as she had to, and she shrivelled in my arms, but she had asked that wonderful question, she had smiled—please, please let me believe that she had smiled!—and I looked down on her tiny face, now so terrible *empty*, and understood at last what she had really given me. *And forgive us our. . .*

I felt a tingling, a touch, an icy sliver of movement inside me, and looked up weeping and proud and finally free into the hunger in Alain's eyes.

The End

Mouse Diary

by
Dan Wilson

She pencilled in the name IN BLOCK CAPITALS, the name of a faulty vending machine which served her wrong in frailty I confide. Maxine's tits lolloped solemnly to and fro, slipping out her bra without her prior knowledge. To look without touching pained me so, despite my deep misgivings. She had not given express permission to anybody regarding mammary ogling, her ageing orbs carry the weight of great educational burden: A Level psychology. As her number one case study, I fled to the canteen with a real sense of self-import to discuss my perversions with the chef.

Christo the chef took no nonsense from the goofy toothed stream of consciousness I emitted. He told me to hold a saucepan aloft thus giving him license to hurl Ragu pasta sauce everywhere. Throughout this ordeal I daydreamed about the vending machine whose innards I'd stripped out earlier and replenished with a chest level pinhole camera. My curious nature led me to hitherto unexplored pastures. Drugs can be ever so disorientating—and I am surprisingly conservative in my views; I assert that they severely hamper poise, conduct and 'carriage', much to the detriment of one's potential of contributing to society at large. I often frown at my father, who disagrees with me on this point.

II

"It's all just a game to you", said I, recovering in hospice after being broken-legged by an off-duty police officer.

My dad mumbled something about the birds and the bees before sodding off back to his adulterous liaison with his secretary.

The policeman, despite reaching orgasm down my best cardigan, was furious about my goofy teeth denting his bulbous cockhead. Jesus, some people are never satisfied. He said that although it was pain-less, the aesthetics had been altered without consent or something. Somewhere in my back pocket was the vending machine service manual. Tentatively, I avoided anal insertion by a combination of distraction and rigidity of conduct. Perhaps this had infuriated him by means of rear denial, or rather the fear of him seeing the service manual and putting two and two together fortified by frigidity. Some people are sick.

Natasha Kaplinsky was a worthwhile substitute for the leering Jon Snow. She whispered to me sweet nothings about a suicide bomber who killed four and maimed dozens; encoded within this report were inner truths concerning mine and Natasha's soul consuming relationship. It is easy to feel guilty about all the suffering in the world with Natasha enshrined on the cathode fishbowl—making me feel loved for just once in my life. Sucking policemen will never be a replacement for true love. Enjoyable as it is to witness them quake in uniformed bliss, they never hug me, only cradle my head with uncertainty as I partake in the ungodly binding. For all my substantial contravention of local bylaws it is surprising and generous of them to grant me such a get-out-clause. They know of my severe submissiveness and fear of enclosed prison cells, exploiting this at their leisure. But perhaps this was all a dream? Drugs again, you see. Let this be a lesson to you. All I know is that what followed during my recovery is absolutely real . . .

Π

Some plaster-brained animal rights activists appeared on my mum's patio, annoyingly, hindering my difficult masturbations. She smiled at me: Natasha Kaplinsky. If I went outside and bludgeoned to death some animal rights activists, might I one day be the subject of her autocue? I don't fancy her, but she exudes a certain something.

Item one : 9-12 animal rights protesters blocking my view of the lovely chrysanthemums (my mum's)

Item two : I want to kill myself by jumping onto their upright placards. Skewer daydreams.

Item three : The placards contain horrid swearwords.

Item four : There is a man in his twenties wearing a red sweater which he inexplicably removes to reveal a T-shirt with a slogan on it: something something anarchy . . . On my driveway? I hope he takes off his shirt to show off his muscled chest, otherwise it would be boring.

Item five : I threw a petri-dish at a girl he was talking to.

Π

In the absence of my father it is possible to misbehave internally. Regurgitating eggs for the comedy value, short circuiting neural receptors, staring intently at people out the window, stealing other peoples' clothing from the gymnasium and wearing it, etc.

28 Anchor Street; they leave the back door unlocked from 12:45 to 2:00pm weekdays. Felicity the athletic feminist departs from the gym to fetch her salad from Gilbert Road, leaving the door ajar, but shuts the outside gate. The gate is not solid, enabling anorexics and the withered unhealthy to pass between the bars. It's best to take your shoes off and toss them over, since they might get stuck. Good luck. Lo! The tin whistle bloweth, the gristle groweth. Only the most determined of perverts could endure the wager to clothing theft total bonanza. Within the cathedral of self-improvement there are many buxom souls, chunky guys, yoghurt eaters, sweaty folk and self-assured women. On the surface it is a recipe for all sorts of depravity, but thankfully a healthy body makes for a healthy mind (apparently).

Alien intruders are thrown out at reception stage, but the clever aforementioned bypass gives access to all the healthy peoples' clothes! Take them and wrap yourself in hitherto unknown confidences! Rise from loveless slumber to newfound ecstasy! Clutch these optimism drenched fabrics and have comfort! Unfortunately they lock all the doors now and they've installed CCTV. Spoilsports.

Π

In the absence of my mother it is beneficial to misbehave externally. There are twenty or so animal rights protesters on the driveway outside. Some are old, some are young and some wear hooded apparel. For many hours I've watched them shuffle peaceably—thank God—waiting for my parents, no doubt. But what would they think of me? Would they like me? With my bedroom window slightly open, it is possible to discern their infantile chatter. A woman with long grey hair is referred to as 'Liz', and she is talking to a handsome man I mentioned earlier; his name is 'Adam'. There are no attractive women in the crowd (but who cares?). Adam has dark spiky hair, possibly some piercings, pale eyes, a sense of humour (his laughing is audible), a T-shirt bearing an illegible slogan and a red sweater tied sexily around his waist. I genuinely require his red sweater for my research. Does he want a cup of tea? I'd give him my favourite mug. Willing him to peel off his shirt drains so much mental energy that it's hard to maintain balance. Shall I be a hero and set free my mother's lab mice? Perhaps Adam will hold me to arraign for my parents' misdeeds . . . Perhaps Adam will hold me to censure for my possibly unnatural interest in his body . . . Well, at least he'll hold me. I'm not a pervert, I'm a dreamer. Likewise, I'm not gay, I'm just bored. Most painfully, I cannot face this mob because I'm too nervous. I wish they'd all fuck off except Adam. He seems nice.

Π

Offended are the whelks on which the cosmopolitan chew. Business function attendees have the gumption to resume heedless consumption. Headless whelks are angry—my Lord, will you forgive my parents? Spare them from the wrath of the mighty whelk emperor whose tormented minions have endured cosmetic experiments. Be merciful.

Evening became morning and I ventured outside to inspect the earth where the animal rights protesters stood only hours beforehand. Where Adam stood. Adam, will you ever forgive me for my listless lack of concern for animal welfare? I will never defile Adam's body for the sake of cosmetic products for women whose ephemeral whimsies amount to nothing but slutty eugenics. Or for medical research, which serves nothing but the continuation of human existence, pulling with it all its vanity and misery into future ages. With my apathy deferred to lacklustre trouser pounding, I commit my heart to Adam's image and his principles. Mice, whelks, rats and hamsters are plentiful—Adam, however, is not. Whilst it is harmless to fantasise about Adam; his body, his ideals and his red sweater—it would be unthinkable to even introduce myself to him. Any bodily congress between us (perish the thought), consensual or otherwise, will surely be inharmonic and our theoretical intercourse would be devoid of passion due to ideological and temperamental incompatibilities. The mutual allowances required to bridge our differences rest dead centre on a disembowelled rodent, whelk or unspecified animal intestine. I would have to ornament my speech to impress him—he would probably not enjoy my underclassy, consonantless talk. Adam, we spent a day together but you didn't

see or hear me whispering to you from behind my net curtains. You stood on the very driveway I played on as a child. Cunt.

Π

Emotionally crippled by the internal brain-jazz, the clutter of the mildly homosexual week is compressed, filtered and converted to blood and semen. Knives, tissues, private moments and Natasha Kaplinsky jabbering in the corner. I don't fancy her. Her looks make me jealous. Actually, she might even be wearing make-up tested on animals. Suddenly mother and father returned home from their conference two days late. It was very difficult for me to fix up and reignite an acceptably steadfast pilot-light of heterosexuality. If Kaplinsky won't fire up the neurones, who will? What a pathetic state of affairs. I wanted Adam to return, but I've resigned myself to the fact that I'll never even obtain his red sweater, let alone his attentions. Distractions. Anyway, why should newslady Natasha Kaplinsky's sub-softcore, nay, nothingcore delivery of news titbits titillate anybody anyway? What is most certainly needed to permeate the distracted sex-drive is full-on hardcore. It was reported in the newspaper that Natasha Kaplinsky herself was about a launch a Global Breast Cancer Awareness Campaign at the Arts Club in London. London is hugely scary, and only insane people go there. Wouldn't it be nice to affix a miniature wireless camera to a radio-controlled moth? Zig-zagging across the borough with digital inelegance to feed me transmissions from this Arts Club. Valuable straight porn. Although Natasha Kaplinsky is a respectable woman; she would probably remain fully clothed, even for Breast Cancer Awareness parties. It would be a waste of a bionic moth.

Π

It is most peculiar how love typically instils great amplified emotions of happiness, sorrow and fixation, despite any attempts at self-distraction. To an uninvolved party, I'm sure this all comes across zested with pungent embarrassment.

Hmmm. If I advertised a false claim

that my parents were preparing to execute a cute monkey next Monday, will Adam see fit to return? If I arranged such a desperate deed, would it yield fruit? Why did Adam appear on the driveway initially? Something must have set that protest off. The protesters did nothing except hold placards, drink beverages from flasks and shiver. Perplex, perplex, perplex— perpetual periphrastic perhapses. Perhaps perhaps perhaps Adam was there because he knows of my existence? It seems too perfect that the most gorgeous man I'd ever seen should appear to me amidst the scene of an animal rights protest right outside my house directed towards my parents. Perhaps he sent the death threat to my dad which I intercepted so fortuitously? If so, then he intimately understands my father's strange temper when matters of differing sexualities are placed before him, and thus my situation—so much so, that it all seems too orchestrated by a higher intelligence to be the result of chance. I sensed hatred in that message of looming murder which, oddly enough, triggered tumescence by its sheer outrageousness. Adam must surely want to degrade me, yet I would delight in assenting to his motivations, whatever their pretence. It would be delightful to pleasure Adam ideologically, or otherwise. Adam must surely love me.

I turn on the radio to distract myself only to hear this song:

"I used to think maybe you loved me, now baby I'm sure;
And I just can't wait 'till the day when you knock down my door.
Now every time I go to the mailbox, gotta hold myself down,
'Cos I just can't wait 'till you say that you're coming around.
I'm walking on sunshine, wooah,
I'm walking on sunshine, wooah,
I'm walking on sunshine, wooah,
and don't it feel good?!"

Cutting my wrists to the beat I am suffused with confusion. If Adam doesn't love me I'll murder him happily, presumably.

With nauseating cynicism the collapse of fecundity demolishes all moral fail-safes. A false cadence accents existing disappointments miserably, throwing up fear, dread, abominable self-doubt and profound detachment to all humanity. "I'm walking on sunshine, wooah". Then a sight catches the attention: something from the night before, perhaps. Eggs erupted on a neighbour's Vauxhall Astra with flour toppings; what dismal baker could ever construct such backward attempts at pastry compounding? Did these eggs come from a so-called battery farm where hens are maltreated? Why have they strained their sphincters to give us eggs only for us to steal them and hurl them mindlessly at vehicles? We, or certain swathes of the human race at least, are truly worse than animals—being ungrateful to those that suffer the straining peristalsis of egg outputting. Jesus knows the hens fantasise about regaining their freedom; Adam's manly arms scoop five live hens from the rigours of battery-hen frameworks and steel impedimenta. His warm red sweater blissfully envelops the hens during the escapade. I wish Adam would do the same for me, for I am also a slave to Tesco, yet my blinkered antennae quiver as if anticipating diabolical consequences, such an act of selfless heroism misinterpreted as a prelude to sexual activity. Embarrassing ideas. Most certainly though, this is not the case, and I vouch my heterosexual linearity through an admixture of swearing and time-determined windows of ferocious masturbation at my shrine to twentysomething gymnasium-goers; items of clothing, television stills printed onto acetate and other ephemera associated toward heterosexual homogeny. This is not filth, but clean and sensible hobbies. It may be necessary to cancel all library subscriptions as certain 'deviant' books are most likely flagged and monitored.

Π

No more withdrawals. Withstanding nausea wrought by issue desk suspicion; suspicion must piss onward, ever wary of these social outcasts reading up on urophagia or what-have-you, hidden in the silence and sanctity of town libraries. Do you see then? See men? Seethe men, now. According to my research, everybody's semen tastes slightly different, but most often smelling vaguely of bleach. People who smoke a lot of marijuana have rather pungent cheesy semen, whilst chocolate-eaters' reproductive juice is very thick and velvety, like salty mousse. I am prepared for anything and everything in this chaotic world in which we live. Let me recount a recollection: a Pyrex dish was dropped from the second floor balcony killing a 19-year-old girl smoking below, near the student union building. This happened at Broxbourne College in the early 21st century. There was a peculiar smell the next day, on the very spot where the girl had died . . . It was like bleach, disinfectant, old pants, socks, sweat, meat and soap. This smell is the scent equivalent of how semen tastes (without wishing to belittle the magnitude of the sombre events linked to that smell). I got told off for sniffing the paving slab. How come they didn't let me pore over the paving slab? I bet Jessica Fletcher (of 'Murder, She Wrote') would have been allowed to inspect the scene of the mystery. At lunchtime I pretended to fall over onto the deathspot to catch another breath of this evocative bouquet. It is very very reminiscent of clingy, snot-like semen coating the innermost depths where my throat ends and my heart begins. I explained this to any students who happened to stare, and in their eyes gleamed the truest empathy albeit shackled by youthful obligations to show defensiveness in the presence of uncool stuff. The minutes ticked by and the aroma of pastry from the canteen soon cancelled the dream.

Typically, people with blue eyes have semen flavoured as sea-water. My mate said so.

Π

I would cheerfully gatecrash a nightclub and commit genocide if I wasn't so painfully shy. What's more, it would be utterly embarrassing to appear on the front page of the local newspaper beside Reverend Humphries' unfashionably dainty 'Thought of the Day'. So it's best to show some restraint.

My mum phoned home to ascertain my mental state and I made up a story about a burglar buggering me in the dead of night, but she was very liberal and didn't care. Or perhaps she wields that motherly intuition that can identify truth, fiction and friction, and just feigns ignorance so as not to hurt my feelings.

Because I'm allegedly a twat, it seemed logical to dance maniacally to a Casio keyboard demo-tune for the remainder of the day. Natasha Kaplinsky is becoming irritating; loading all the world's troubles onto my shoulders. Her half-baked attempt to balance the awful news of bombs, knifings, sex attacks, shootings, intolerance and tantrums with the obligatory funny news at the climax is like performing cunnilingus (a different kind of language, I imagine) whilst she is in a bad mood. Correspondingly, it is not unusual to feel used and wretched after being told about a biscuit factory in Dagenham which motivates its staff by handing them CD players and Abba CDs; this news suffixed onto a report on gangland killings and mutilated bodies. It is not surprising, therefore, that my mood veers from the murderous to the personable, from the remorseful to the sarcastic, from the abominably vengeful to the cockthirsty.

Π

Slipping the two forefingers down my throat during breakfast, it is extremely difficult to judge whether I could ever suck penii competently without suffering choking or lockjaw. This realisation neither bothers nor disappoints, it is merely whimsy borne of boredom, apathy, disaffection and mimicry of my slut cousin Sonia. We met by pure chance last Saturday on Anchor Street when I was shopping for sponge and foam. By force of habit I always aim to deflect the ceaseless volley of criticism levelled at my whoring cousin Sonia with upturned dustbin lids and false smiles. Our moods were identical: upset and upset. Someone had called her a "user" (again), whilst I had only just realised that 'comfort shopping' for sponge will never fill the empty void of my life. As Sonia's waterworks began mass-producing teardrops I mopped up her face with an industrial fire-retardant sponge purchased earlier. It smudged her mascara disastrously, but at least it stifled the misery that threatened to engulf our conversation. Likewise, I also mopped my own tears away with a separate pink sponge in my other hand. Time stood perfectly still as we buried our tear-sodden faces in sponge simultaneously on Anchor Street amidst the midday bustle. Although, as I held the sponges in both our faces it wasn't entirely certain how long I should cover her face. I peeped over my sponge to see if she was still appreciating the sponge. She was. Twenty minutes later I had another peek, but she had vanished! For a split second it seemed as though the sponge had absorbed her entirely. Standing static with my face covered and the industrial fire-retardant sponge held aloft in my puny hand for nobody must've looked very silly indeed, and lonely. Why on earth did she disappear without telling me to lower the sponge from her face? I tried to think back if there were any instances of Sonia's voice I may have unconsciously overlooked during those twenty minutes, but no, there weren't. It seemed very rude of her. Perhaps her tormenters were right all along; that she is simply a "user". She used my sponge without so much as a "thank you". Anger and embarrassment boiled through my stomach walls, flooding my hollow heart with hot stomach acid and my liquefied breakfast. In fury I hurled my pink sponge to the gutter and set about hunting her down with the other industrial tear-soaked sponge, which I gripped menacingly, squeezing out Sonia's tears onto the tarmac.

Through the myriad shops, pubs, cafes, taverns and alleys, I darted wildly, grunting when environments failed to yield my slut cousin Sonia. The rest of the day was spent in this loop: searching for Sonia—user of sponges and supreme bicycle of Hertfordshire. There was no conclusion or knot to bind the day neatly to the brain's catalogue of straight, bright, dark, gay, exciting, dismal, or plain fatiguing remembrances. Painfully, the day had started to draw to a close with me bawling camply in the cloakroom of Cameron & Guy's hair salon, as scissors fell to the floor.

For bisexuals, hairdressing 'business' partners Cameron & Guy were surprisingly unfriendly to me. On the hit gameshow 'Supermarket Sweep' a sexually ambiguous man named Dale Winton treats all his contestants, and even his viewers, with warmth and affection, no matter what their backgrounds or circumstances. I was hoping either Cameron or Guy might possibly have conformed to this bubbly stereotype and comfort me with tissue, cuddles, there-theres and possibly a 'sympathy makeover' (regularly doled out to women or men with low self-esteem on daytime TV shows). Alas, there was none of this fabulous fuss-fuss—they simply glared at me as I wailed in mental agony. Paradoxically, their inactivity provoked me into wailing louder, rendering me in all likelihood still more unapproachable. It wasn't right. Somebody dropped a pair of scissors (as I mentioned earlier) yet this lacked a complementary cry of "oh butterfingers" accompanied by limp-wristed flailing; this all indicated something was utterly amiss. Where was the love? Just like a beached jellyfish I writhed through the frosting of loose hair on the floor, then I became a plough snaking over the increasing concentrations of mixed tresses and fibres. Underneath a shelving unit piled with haircare products I made my nest, deploying my industrial sponge at the entrance like a flag—asserting my government over this new found cubbyhole. Hands on hips, the hairdressers swarmed around my nest attempting to 'lift' the shelving unit. I buried myself in the hair cuttings before a bulky yet attractive Cypriot man wrenched me out and ejected me angrily.

The merest touch from another man sends shivers of inverted passion darting to initialise the body for imminent roughage; even the gentlest prod of a college tutor reverberates and sustains itself. But to be carelessly lifted from the familiar suck of gravity and hurled out a hair salon by a cocksure stranger is tantalisingly near to pure reset: blissful rebooting. Jesus, to what new category of cognisance does the ecstasy derived from being manhandled by another man belong? Does the odd necessity to be physically repositioned by another male stem from the uprooting of traditional female complicity under masculine forcefulness? Aye, we must embrace feminism, simultaneously resolving our ancestral inequities by obeying their every demand; expressly disavowing any violations upon the female demeanour and approaching our worship of femininity only through self-flagellation in meek and lowly constraint. As the few channels of communication between genders deteriorate, we find ourselves fawning, gawping and dribbling over weathergirls, hostesses or newsreaders without comprehending the messages they deliver. The Goddesses on high, held in constant satisfaction through electro-mechanical stimuli, cast their narrowed eyes over the minging morass of men wheezing for glory, climbing atop each other, and by the sixteen moons of Jupiter they will flame and oppress the wretched hunks for thy is the kingdom, the power and glory, forever and ever.

Is it any wonder that inter-male fumblings grow more furious and splenetic as the Goddesses deny their affections toward the vilest gender? Whatever physical contact we catch—accidentally or otherwise—should be cherished and integrated into imaginary relationships we keep to ourselves. Yet I shall sprint to the newsagent to examine top shelf publications and periodicals; the one place the Goddesses fail to govern. And oh Jesus! Opening the magazines, I see images of the Goddesses being abused; maltreated. Rear entry is so unnecessary. Why don't the men just interact with each other rather than inflicting this pain upon the Goddesses? Agony can clearly be seen in their faces. Begrudgingly I do consider volunteering myself to be ramming recipient by way of diverting their brutality away from the Goddesses' delicate sphincters. Lest their mascara eyes may favour me for saving them, like Jupiter eating the solar system's crap. For all these years amongst the cherry groves of arcane logic, I have festered charity infused boils, namely yearnings to supplant womankind's suffering with my own. To these alpha-heterosexual big-bollocked stallions I could become 'whipping boy' or fuck receptacle, so subsequently the Goddesses would see me as a saviour of the nicest creed —sparing them of the degrading, relentlessly shuddering onslaught from the barbarians. Nobody likes barbarians—that's why we have universities to subdue such primitivism.

Π

A few weeks ago some men hijacked some aeroplanes and rammed them into iconic American landmarks. It was interesting to note that Channel Five's morning news that very day, hours before this hijacking happened, carried a news segment on 'sexercise'—a new American phenomenon where exercise is amalgamated with stripping and sexiness. Sadly, stripping is a very cruel act because it implies 'look but don't touch' and this creates widespread frustration. Amalgamating the discordant concepts of self-improvement, self-degradation and self-pity is physically impossible, and if it did perchance occur, time and space would be severely damaged—as if twinning light and darkness. This is probably one of the reasons why the hijacking took place.

Now, the TV show entitled 'Sex and the City' no longer features the New York World Trade Centres in its opening titles, yet the women portrayed in the show still insist on promoting one-night stands in painful scenes. Their city came under unexpected attack resulting in unprecedented death and panic, so perhaps they need to shake the thoughts from their mind by purposeful self-degradation. I cannot help but wonder that if the hijackers had sexually encountered the characters from 'Sex and the City', none of this unpleasantness would have ever taken place—that is, the terrorist attacks and the mentally terrorising TV show (which, admittedly, can be switched off unlike unswitchoffable terrorism). However, this melting-pot alternative history is the stuff of interdimensional daydreams. Anyway . . . The very act of forcing a cavity into one inappropriate solid object in order to accommodate another solid object glorified through speed is embarrassingly sub-sexual, not to mention the rape of fetishised icons. This act of wilfully determined ham-fisted destruction amounts to nothing but a mere adolescent's tantrum of the crevice-fixated boy variety. Having attended an all-boys' secondary school, I can vouch that, when roused, certain alpha-heterosexual testosterone filled bullies can be very violent and scary, hence the term 'terrorism' attributed to the recent attack. At school however, such boys' appetites and tempers were quelled in the toilets where they fellated each other. I was told never to tell anybody this information.

Π

Wistfully I inspect (nay, sniff) the crazy paving of my mum and dad's driveway where the animal rights activist named Adam once protested against my parents' mouse-splicing antics. The sillystring (sillystring is a registered trademark) these banshees untidily ejaculated has been all but washed away by the recent spell of bad weather. But still I sprawl starfish-like on the moist craziness, imagining what it must be like to be a tiny chipping jammed snugly in the chunky tread of Adam's futuristic boots. Perhaps he'll waggle a lollystick or twig betwixt the grooves to set me loose, cast back to the boring crazy paving like an unloved barnacle. Tears fill my eyes and oesophagus, causing a rush of tragic lovelorn vomit to fill my mouth. As I writhe in agonising gay pain, the bile ebbs away, only to return seconds later reinforced by the two Penguin chocolate bars I ate earlier as a mark of respect to the disappearance of the twin towers in New York. I also ate a Yorkie, but luckily that stayed down. The brown liquid projectile Penguin bile lent an attractive gloss to my nextdoor neighbour's tuft of hydrangeas. Suddenly, with the flicker of a net curtain the neighbour was outside screaming Scottish obscenities. She was in her seventies, yet very lively. I promptly explained that old cliché that "you can never have sex with who you truly love". The funny look she dispensed almost made me wonder if she got the wrong idea.

Π

I often think about what it must be like to be a woman. Women can not only pleasure themselves in multiple areas, but can also accommodate the penis of a man they love inside a specially designed cavity which is sensitive and interesting. It is man's latent need to create his own cavity which leads to wanton violence, damage to the integrity of softer static objects, subtractive physical processes and hollowing out baguettes. However, these acts are merely alternatives to fornication: the actualisation of sustained object crashing. Some women are particularly loath to comply in this utterly unsophisticated penetration (outwardly tidy as it appears), and these ones are collectively referred to as "feminists". Wisely, they seek to avoid the carnal pipe games, and internally cancel any dregs of penile hunger, instead adopting electro-mechanical streamlined plastic harmonically tuned alternatives. The growth of hard-line feminist ideology has seen increasing numbers of men regressing to these infantile acts of frustration. Feminism is rife among animal activist circles, and it's no coincidence that such collectives play host to some very very silly men indeed. Conversely, scientists, researchers and vivisectionists are, by nature, quite introverted university educated people— susceptible to the ramming of bullish men. Likewise, the children of these professional workers may also display a certain softness. Adam may exploit my softness at his will.

Π

There were more protests. My mum used to close the curtains when rowdy protesters had gathered outside, although they were still audible. If anything, the loss of vision heightened my fear and my heart rate. With only the sound of their often full-bodied invectives to accompany my frantic tea stirring, my mother would often bark random biological jargon in ridiculously slurred parlance to distract my aching heart. The pages of the Daily Mail were turned very loudly and slowly on these occasions. Often I queried my psychic abilities to determine if Adam was outside, and occasionally I visualised him urinating against the front door as a matter of principle. However, what he probably doesn't know is that I'd joyously bathe in his warm golden humour, thus welcoming in his disrespect and anger. Adam would understand that when I degrade myself in his thrall, I am at the same time presenting him with a scenario denied to him by his feminist cohorts. He may also feel joy that the wretched progeny of freelance vivisectionists basks in his bladder's mean-spirited piss squirtings. Leave the shy scientists to continue their research into cancer cures and asthma vaccines and direct your stream at me, Adam. When this union is actuated there will be no need for Adam to wallow in angst under the animal rights pretence anymore, in fact, he would find himself able to cross the breach into my home and have tea and supper with me and my parents, and pleasant conversation will resound throughout the house! And Adam should understand that, by and large, the animals feel no pain since they are tranquilised. I am also tranquilised through sniffing solvents and ingesting anti-depressants. Adam may now sink his penis into me.

Π

Why don't the animal rights activists terrorise cancer sufferers or children with a sweet tooth? Testing drugs and food additives is sensible isn't it? Oh God, what am I talking about? I have truly gone insane.

The women are the problem; robbing me of peacefulness—having a monopoly on all the most brilliant cocks. I rot in stagnant depression as Kaplinsky prods me through the cathode ray. She knows what she has done. The BBC bias their news reports ever so slightly in favour of "the people". Unfortunately the so-called "people" are very ignorant. Reports of public unrest are conveyed with a twinkly-eyed sympathy, therefore encouraging activists to wreak their havoc. Kaplinsky knows her make-up has been tried and tested on many lesser faces; would she settle for anything less? All women of this creed congeal in cosmetic majesty casting a spell of homosexuality downwards. They know that tough titty breaks the baby's teeth. By way of diversion I perform impromptu surgery on my body with my parents' vivisection equipment. The laboratory mouse does not know nor understand what processes are occurring upon itself, but it will always seek to escape pain through paths of least resistance—now made manifest as recorded hard biological data. It follows Gaynor's Law —"I will survive". No matter how unpleasant the low resistance exit, it will be hankered for always. Behind the scenes, researchers will be recording data pertaining to this low resistance exit and awaiting outcomes.

Π

In that familiar hospital days later, my mum gave me a cheque for a thousand pounds as consolation for acting as unwilling participant in the special drug trial that she oversaw. She apologised for causing my perceptions of the world to become confused, but said that we are all out of debt now. This tallied up with my conclusion that the paths of least resistance are always taken whether we are conscious of it or not, and all feelings of love, grief, anger, regret, spite, lust, bewilderment, revelation, happiness, sadness, pain, joy are nothing but prominent yet illusory portraits hung attractively along that path.

The End

Queer And Loathing On The Yellow Brick Road

by
Deb Hoag

The first time I saw Glinda the Good, she looked yummy enough to eat. But I was was too young—just a babe in arms, really—so she wouldn't let me. Instead, she sent me back to Kansas. Time passed. Uncle Henry died of a stroke out in the fields, and Auntie Em was right behind him. She finally had that heart-attack she was always threatening me with. Co-dependent or what?

As soon as Auntie Em's funeral was over, I hightailed it back to Oz, stopping only for a memorial quickie with Hickory, Zeke and Hunk—call it severance pay. I cut off those frickin' braids, and ditched the gingham for glittery eyeliner, spandex and blood-red acrylic nails. I got a new pair of shoes and threw the ruby slippers in the back of the closet. I was *rockin'* that stupid Yellow Brick Road.

Glinda and I have been together ever since she saw me "strollin' the brick", as the Bawdy Babes Social Club calls it. She was a little disturbed at my profession, but,

hey, by that time I was nobody's baby. Things have been changing in Munchkinland, though, and I was considering hitting a faraway part of town for a while and getting in some serious shopping until the weather changed.

I cast a discontented glance at Glinda, who was passed out on the couch. She'd grown into a boozy, cantankerous old broad, with bulgy eyes due to her thyroid condition, and was headed for wicked witch-hood at double march unless she changed her tune pretty quick. As I studied her, she roused a little, muttering and trying to scrape her hair out of her eyes without moving her hungover head. Since I met her, she's swallowed an ocean of banana daiquiris, one blender-full at a time. That and magic dust were all she lived on.

Before she could get it together enough to demand another quart or two of booze, there was a knock at the door. I looked out the peephole and saw a group of dark-skinned Munchkins out there, all dressed in black. They looked like a bunch of Gary Coleman commandos. Usually, a visit by one of the Munchkin guilds was something to be avoided like the plague, but with Typhoon Glinda getting ready to blow, they didn't look so bad. I stepped out on the porch and closed the door behind me.

"Hey, girl," said the leader. "We represent the Malcolm X Order."

He paused, and after a minute of awkward silence, I blinked at him. "So, don't you guys have a song or something?"

"Nah, girl, that's old school. We write angry letters and do sit-ins. We hear your . . . friend has been dissing our people. We don't like it. That needs to stop." He looked at me meaningfully.

Just then the door burst open and a groggy Glinda half staggered, half fell out onto the porch. She glared at the Munchkins. "Wahthahell ju guys wan? Imm busy!"

Yeah, she was busy alright—busy pickling her liver.

"Look, you oppressor honky dike, We ain't gonna take anymore shit off of you. Making the Lolly Pop Guild cater your election party for free, demanding 'ludes from the Lullaby League. Those people get good money for their services. From now on, you wanna dance, you gotta pay."

Glinda glared at him, then turned a suspicious eye on me. She was starting to focus. Uh-Oh. She gets really mean when she focuses. "Why'm I the honky dike? What about her? Why isn't she a honky dike?"

The head Malcolm Munchkin looked me over slowly, and smiled lasciviously. "First of all, you're the one who's dangerous; she couldn't fight her way out of a paper bag. Second of all, she's easy. Just remember, leave the Munchkins alone, unless you want to find my boot up your ass bigtime, bitch."

He pointed a finger at Glinda and mimed pulling a trigger. There was some snickering from the Malcolms behind him. Glinda was speechless with fury. All she could do was sputter. Every little droplet of spit morphed into some kind of misshapen bug that slithered away into the azaleas.

It was kinda impressive. I gave her a sultry look. "You want to go inside and do what comes naturally?"

She grimaced. "What I want is a blender full of banana daiquiris. And don't get stingy with the rum."

Do you believe that? I made her banana daiquiris alright. And while I was in there, cranking the blender, I spit in her frickin' rum.

II

Things were quiet for a day or so, but that kind of ominous quiet that portends bad things. I looked out the back door while I waited for Toto to finish crapping in the neighbors' rose bushes. I could see Little Miss Manners next door watching from her window and ready to bust her fat little gut, but she was too afraid of Glinda to do anything.

"Hey, wimp, grow a set of balls," I yelled at her across our yards.

The shutter snapped shut with an audible snap, and then I could hear her shouting at her husband about something totally different. What a lame-ass.

Toto was done, so I whistled him in and closed the door on the high-pitched hausfrau. Poor hubby! Maybe I'd pop by sometime when the missus wasn't around and offer him a little neighborly comfort . . .

. . . and nearly bumped into Glinda when I turned around. I jumped nearly a foot; she'd been out cold in front of the magic ball —which got great reception, by the way— when I'd gone to let Toto out.

"What the hell were you doing?" Her voice, which used to be high and clear as a bell, had first gone smoky, and then deeper still, until she sounded like she'd been gargling with Draino. "Were you flirting with that guy next door?" She took a brutal drag on her cigarette. "Because those Munchkins are *not* that well built. Take it from me."

That really pissed me off. I dragged a hand through my hair, which did massive damage to my spiky, cheeky 'do, by the way. Which pissed me off even more. I'd paid good money—actually, not *money,* so to speak—for that haircut, and for the dark chocolate-cherry color that went on it.

"That is so *totally* over the rainbow. I was bitching out that stupid little cow next door. And how the hell do you know how Munchkins are built? You said you'd never been with a Munchkin when we got together. So when . . . "

My voice trailed off as I realized the implications of what I was saying. "You Jezebel! Have you been cheating on me behind my back? What the hell is wrong with you?"

Glinda smirked. "I can't help it if you're gullible, kid. Make me a batch of daiquiris. And this time, don't spit in the rum."

I stood blinking at her scrawny form. She looked more like Hymen the drag queen than Good Witch Glinda. What was it that made drunken old women invariably choose dingy satin with molting feathers? Before I could answer myself, there was a knock at the front door. Glinda looked back and glared at me. "If it's those fuckin' Munchkins again, tell 'em to get the hell off my property before I turn them all into toads or mushrooms or something. I hate those little pricks."

She went in and sat down on the couch with a huff of anger.

She'd lost a slipper on her way through the house, and looked ridiculous, smoking skinny cigars in an emerald green holder, in a grimy satin robe with a big skirt and feathered neckline and sleeves. She was kicking her slippered foot back and forth like she was wishing someone's ass was in front of it. The slipper, one of those puffy donkey ones, looked like it was going to jump to safety any second. Feathers were floating through the air in tempo with her kicks.

"Really, Glinda, can't you just get happy?"

She didn't answer. I sighed and went to the door.

There was nobody there. I was turning to go back in when someone hissed at me from the bushes. "Psst! Turn the porch light out—I can't afford to be seen here. But I have important news. Can I come in?"

I looked back at Glinda, that two-timing bitch, and then shrugged. "Sure, whatever." Never rains but it pours. I saw the hausfrau looking out her window again, so I flipped her the bird and then hit the light switch on the wall as well, so the living-room was plunged into darkness.

I heard a thump and a muffled "Fuck!" and winced. She must have been in the middle of crossing the room when I turned out the lights. A small figure slipped by me, and I shut the door and hit the light switch.

The little man looked more like a mole than a Munchkin. He blinked and shuffled in the light. "I . . . "

There was another thump, followed by another muffled curse. We both turned to see Glinda rubbing a shin, while balancing a lit cigarette and a pitcher full of daiquiris. The end table was now a banana bush. Damn! I liked that table. When Glinda got to the couch, she dropped down on it hard, and glared at us.

"I represent the Society of Snitches and Sell Outs," he said.

"What the hell do you want?" Glinda had decided to be her usual charming self. "It's three o'clock in the morning, dammit."

Actually, it was about nine-thirty, but I didn't bother to tell her that.

"Well, I have a song, and everything." He cleared his throat, but before he could sing a single note, Glinda cut him off.

"If you just came here to exercise your pipes, you can get right the hell out of my house, half-pint. I've got better things to do."

"No, no," he said hastily. "I've come here with an important message, oh Glinda, Good Witch of the North."

"What's that, tiny?"

He coughed into his hand, one of those polite, not-really-a-cough kinda coughs. Glinda rolled her bulgy eyes and reached for her bag. She pulled out five bucks and handed it to the Snitch. He looked at it, looked back at Glinda, whose face could curdle milk, and decided five was enough.

"The Guerilla Guild has put together a plot to overthrow you, Glinda the Good. The Malcolm Order, the Lolly Pop Guild, the Lullaby League and the Castro Commissars are committed, and we think the Stalin Society and possibly the Fascist Funsters are about ready to sign on."

"The Munchkins? Think they can overthrow *me*?" To our amazement, she burst into laughter.

It took her nearly a minute to get herself back under control. Her laughter sounded like a rusty chainsaw, and she didn't stop until it triggered a coughing fit. Sounded like she was ready to hawk up a lung. Then her face changed and she looked at the snitch and hollered, "Get the hell out of my house, you lying sack of shit!"

He blinked and stepped back, then looked fearfully at the door. "But . . . but . . . "

"Brag about your butt on your own time, shorty." She pointed an imperious finger his way and magic sparked off the tip. Snitch made his decision. Glinda in his face was scarier than whatever might be waiting for him outside. He flung the door open and rushed out onto the porch, then stopped, trying to figure out what way to go. In that second he paused, a shot rang out from the dark, and Snitch's head exploded all over the deck.

Glinda stood and walked over to survey the mess sourly. "Go out there and clean that shit up. And get my five bucks back while you're at it."

Π

What I actually did was drag Snitchy into the neighbors' rose bushes, and then hose off the porch. The next morning, I was hanging out in the kitchen, waiting eagerly to hear the hausfrau's screams of terror, when Glinda came stumping in.

"Geezus, Glinda. It's nine a.m. You can't really be looking for booze this early, can you? And good morning, by the way."

"Pack a bag. We're off to see the Wizard."

"The Wizard? You mean good old Johnny one-note? What the hell for? I got stuff to do. I can't just take off on a moment's notice."

Glinda scowled. "You're either with me or against me. Make up your mind."

I packed even quicker than I had gotten rid of Snitch.

Π

We didn't bother with any of that "follow the yellow brick road" bullshit this time. We traveled in a big bubble that smelled faintly of rum and bananas, and arrived in Emerald City before lunch. I begged off when we got there and went to go get my roots touched up and a couple of tubes of Embraceable You siren red lipstick. We agreed to meet up at the palace when I was done.

When I got back to the palace, they were still yacking. Oz looked even more like a disreputable old hustler than he had the last time I saw him. As I walked in, I heard him whining, "But, Glinda, you know I'm not a real wizard!"

Glinda replied sourly, "You better pony up some balls fast, you old fraud. Or find something that can help in one of those big trunks of yours. Because there's a tornado coming our way, and this time we might all get smashed."

Oz's eyes flicked over to where I stood in the doorway. For just a moment, his eyes went unfocused. Was that a line of drool? Ewe! Glinda looked at him and then at me, then socked him in the shoulder. He pulled himself up quick, emitting a small yelp of pain, and started rubbing the shoulder he had hit, looking sullen.

Glinda scowled. "You've known her since she was ten, for Christ's sake. I'm a marked woman, here. Stop thinking with your dick and figure out how to help us."

Us? "Uh, you guys? You look like you're still pretty busy. I think I'll just go and see if Naughty Nails is still open. Nobody gives a French tip like the Manicure Mob."

Glinda waved me absently away.

Last I heard was Oz saying, "Something out of my trunks, eh? Maybe. Just maybe. Hold that thought for a second. I've got to go take a wiz."

II

My first—well, actually, my only—thought was to call and beg Ozma to help me. She was only a year older than I was, and had been raised as a boy, so she understood what it was like to walk both sides of the street, so to speak. Last time I had seen her she was still a little confused by the whole thing, but who wouldn't be? Maybe I could hide out with her until I found the silver lining in all this.

I tried her land line, but didn't get an answer, so all I could do was leave a message. She apparently hadn't resolved all those pesky gender identity issues yet. "Hello," she trilled. "You've reached the hotline for Transgender Anonymous. We've missed your call, because we're either out shopping for shoes or bowling, so please leave a message, and a guy or gal—or both—will get back to you soon. Ciao!"

I left a message and my cell number, then went out in search of raspberry chocolate cappuccino and company. Not necessarily in that order.

I was standing in front of a shop run by the Shoe and Boot Society, looking at a hot pair of Jimmy Choo-Choo wedgies—the wedges were fashioned into train engines, and made soft "I think I can" noises with every step—cool or what? My cell phone rang. Ozma, finally!

"Ozma, is that you? I'm am so glad you called. You won't believe what's going on in Munchkinland!"

"I've been hearing rumors, and it's Ozaak, today, if you don't mind."

I should have known by the deep voice.

"Ozaak, I got it. You've heard about it all the way over here in Emerald City?"

"Word travels. I hear Glinda has totally flipped her lid, turned into a complete dictator. Are you okay?"

Briefly, I described what was happening.

"And she came to Oz, instead of

me, huh? That tells you something right there, sweet cheeks. Not good. Not at all."

I can't tell you the relief I had in putting the burden on Ozaak's broad shoulders. "So, you'll do something before anybody else gets killed? I think she's going into holocaust mode—I swear to God."

"I hadn't realized things were in such a crisis state. Let me get a few things together. It's a long way to Tipperary—I mean Munchkinland. You take the high road, right?"

"Yeah," I sighed. I get airsick. "By bubble as usual."

"Chin up, Dorothy. I'll take the low road and still be there by the time you get back."

Feeling better than I had in weeks, I went back to the hotel to wait for Glinda.

Π

We waited until dark to bubble back, Oz traveling with us, along with a carpet bag full of God knows what.

Still, when the bubble landed in our backyard, I saw the snap of blinds on the house next door. The hausfrau had been waiting for us. She must have been burning up the phone lines, because less than ten minutes later, a rock was thrown through our livingroom window, scattering shards of glass everywhere.

"Come on out, White Mamma," it read. Oh, boy, it was the Malcolms again. "Get out of that hell house and apologize for what you been doin', or 20,000 years in Sing-Sing is gonna seem like short time to you."

Glinda turned red and swelled up like a toad when she read it. Oz started looking nervously toward the back door, but he couldn't move half as fast as Glinda when she was pissed off. She grabbed him with one hand and me with the other, and dragged us outside with her to confront the angry mob.

Oz barely had a chance to grab his bag as he passed.

On the porch, Glinda squinted and glared in the light from the torches. There must have been a hundred Munchkins out there, all armed with something or other—from pitchforks to machetes.

"Get the hell off my property," she screamed, veins popping out on her neck. Her hair magically freed itself from the neat waves she had had it done in while in the Emerald City, and now frizzed wildly around her head, strands whipping back and forth like snakes. Her face flickered with strange light, throwing the angles into sharp relief that made her look like one of the undead. And she grew in size until she nearly bumped her head on the ceiling of the porch.

Oz, somewhat emboldened by the sight she made, stepped up to her side and opened his carpet bag.

"What you got in there, old man? Another plastic heart?" It was a scornful voice from the mob, and people began snickering.

"More like a plastic Ozzie semi-automatic," he shouted back, and held it aloft. There was some worried muttering and our audience took a collective step back. Everybody knew how dangerous an Ozzie was—if the bullets didn't get you, the incessant bitching would.

The Malcolms were manning up for battle, when there was a shrill neigh from the edge of the crowd. I shielded my eyes against the flaming torches, and then waved and called out excitedly. "Ozaak! You made it!"

Glinda looked at me in disbelief. "You knew that freak was coming and you didn't tell me?"

I shrugged. "Three on a match, Glinda. I want to survive this in one piece."

Ozaak had dismounted from her

horse, which was currently a strong, manly navy. As per usual when Ozma was in her Ozaak mode, she had completely lost her sense of fashion, and was wearing a ten-gallon hat, plaid shirt, jeans and cowboy boots. I understand the whole transgender thing, I really do. But why does switching off cause her to wear such really horrible outfits? Emboldened by Ozaak's arrival, someone in the mob threw a rock at the porch, narrowly missing Glinda's head. All of a sudden, a sense of style or lack thereof, didn't seem to matter so much. I jumped to the lawn and scrambled to get to Ozaak's side.

"Hey, Ozaak, thanks for coming. If you want, when this is all over, we could have a spa day. And go shopping. My treat!"

Ozaak nodded absently. She might not appreciate my offer now, but once the Ozma side kicked back in, I knew she'd be delighted.

Glinda drew back the hand with the wand in it, and Oz raised his gun. I winced and tried to make myself smaller. Unfortunately, when the entire rest of the crowd is under three feet, I really stand out.

Glinda's wand sizzled, and someone in the front row turned into a sloth. A flaming arrow, a product of the Gay Archer's Guild, landed on the porch by her feet. She raised her arm for another shot, and Oz pulled the Ozzie to his face and took aim.

"Stop!" thundered Ozaak at my side. "As your queen and your . . . queen, I order you to stop this right now!"

"What the hell are you gonna do with that bitch, if we stop? We can't live like this anymore. We want some guarantees." That had to be one of the Malcolms.

Ozaak stepped forward until she reached the porch, and then turned to face the crowd, a grin in her face. "I have a solution that's way better than some stupid guarantee."

"What's that?" said one of the Lolly Pop Guild members suspiciously.

"What is it?" said Glinda and Oz at the same time, distrust in their voices.

"Before Oz left the palace, I went through his bag. And I found *this*!"

"What the hell is that?" someone shouted.

"Oh, shit," muttered Oz, looking for a way off the porch.

"It's a device our Wonderful Wizard picked up at the Technology Exhibit of the Chicago World's Fair of 1893. A shrink ray."

The audience got quiet as they tried to figure out what exactly that meant. Oz's shoulders slumped. Glinda grinned. "You're gonna make these squirts even tinier than they are now?"

Ozaak turned and looked at Glinda and Oz on the porch, and grinned. "No, I'm going to provide you with a little off the cuff sensitivity training."

Before either of them could say anything else, Ozaak squeezed the trigger of the shrink ray. An eerie blue light shot out, enveloping both Glinda and Oz in its strange glow. There was a blinding flash, and then the blue light disappeared. We all looked at the figures on the porch. Glinda and Oz, but different—they were both less than three feet tall.

"Oh, my God," screamed Glinda. Her voice was about two octaves higher, which was a total improvement. "What have you done, you bitch?"

There was scattered giggling from the yard, and then some outright guffaws. Pretty soon, the whole place was rocking with hysterically laughing Munchkins. Ozaak was laughing too, but managed to get it under control enough to call out to the crowd. "Now, who's going to volunteer to help

Glinda and Oz a better understanding of what it means to be a Munchkin?"

A hand here or there went up, but the pickings looked pretty slim. Ozaak frowned. "And every person that volunteers gets a free date with her." She pointed directly at me. I blushed and tried to look cute. Every hand went up—even the guy married to the hausfrau. At least, his hand was up until she saw him and socked him in the gut. I batted my lashes, and tried to figure out how I could make some money on this deal.

"What are we supposed to do?" Oz was whining. "I don't know how to live like a Munchkin."

I smiled, and called from my position in the back of the crowd, "Look for the silver lining. Now you guys can form your own Munchkin gang—how about the League of Duplicitious Dictators?"

The crowd cheered. Oh, yeah. I could definitely make some money off this.

The End

A Shade Of Yellow

by
Alex Dally MacFarlane

My

side .

. . .

The deal . . . Don't forget . . . " Moans, lurid in the summer air, are swallowed by the engines. Each clanks and emits a regular hiss of steam, overlapping beyond the dirty window into cacophony.

Yes, yes, lose yourself, let go, release your mind with the grip, thrust, groan and yes!

Shudders control his body in a brief moment of ecstasy. Then, finished, he pushes up and moves to the side of the bed. A smile curves his lips; the presence is gone from his mind.

The realisation is a hundred times sweeter than sex.

Before work can claim him, he fists the slips of money lying in a nearby drawer and drops them on the girl's bare stomach. The blank look on her face makes him momentarily uncomfortable. Usually they smile, as if there is something more than business passing between them, and most offer a word of thanks. Not she. With drops

of his seed in small beads on the insides of her pale legs, his teeth marks indenting her shoulder, half-clothed from his hasty pursuit of release, she lies still. Grey eyes stare unblinking at the wood-panelled ceiling.

"Thank you." He feels like an awkward teenager with his first woman. Why does that stare unsettle him so much? "I . . . appreciate it." They understand the etiquette, accept that when he is done they must go. But she remains.

Hair as fiercely orange as a sunset, skin as pinkly near-white as the second moon, limbs as supple as a dancer's—aesthetically it is difficult to find better among the Riverside girls. Decay quickly claims them. As she remains unmoving, he decides that inconvenience is a large price to pay for beauty.

"I need you to go now." Blunt, and he regrets it as her pale eyes flicker slightly. Will she cry? She looks young enough to, sometimes.

Not now, please.

He can already feel their presence. More cloying than the steam and sweat of the city, darker than the unlit back alleys and infinitely more threatening. They creep into the room, hugging the corners and skirting-boards. From nowhere comes a screeching sound—chrrkkk you must stop the lifting, you must convince Rulbunn of the perils to the under-city chrrkkk—grating into his brain and slipping out just as quickly.

"They're here," the girl murmurs, and suddenly her eyes snap into focus and her face changes. Gone is the soft, blank palette of youth; staring at him is something far older. "It was wonderful, by the way," she adds. The mockery in her voice makes him momentarily furious, but he sees them creeping closer and the thing he wants most is for her to go.

She dresses, shoves the money in her bra, picks up her bag and leaves the room without further comment. Her footfalls pad-pad away through the apartment and out the main door.

From the chandelier comes a soft gust of air, a murmur of noise like wind brushing through dried-up ivy, and his day's work begins.

П

Your mind is a blank slate. You think, but only of possible clients, money and the food you need. Occasionally you let yourself dream of mansions and being one of the city's great concubines. Less so, lately. Your looks are perfect but for the scar running down your side; they won't take you with that imperfection. Herbal treatments and remedies from the phoney magicians on Riverside have only caused temporary inflammation. The alley feline's mark will linger until death claims you and skin rots.

You will suffice.

П

Thick with rotting food and chemicals, the bright pink of lyril petals bobbing on its surface, the River Effequ rolls torpidly through Retyelnen. On either side rise soot-stained buildings that penetrate the yellow cloud hanging above the sprawling metropolis. Twice the river passes the city's perimeter; twice it casts rippling patterns onto the underbellies of the machines hired by the government to lift Retyelnen above the earth. Then, on either side, after the over-farmed and barren plains, it flows in free curves through endless saraq.

Saraq. The name began as a whisper on the edges. Nearby villages utterly consumed, their heat stolen to fuel the plants' growth. And Retyelnen, the greatest source of heat on the vast northern plain, is their ultimate goal: a feast of furnaces.

Tension hangs in the air, as pervasive and a part of the city's background as the yellow cloud. With the lifting underway, fear has shifted towards nervous anticipation. In Riverside, a district lining a third of the Effequ's western bank within Retyelnen, people's thoughts switch readily to the present. They stare across the river at the simian constructs that daily scrub the richest houses and envy the creatures for their regular employment.

Among them walks Mari, too lost in thought to notice the usual goings-on by the river.

Something changed in the government official's bedroom. She knows that much, even if she can't identify exactly what it was. A strange presence while the man plunged into her like a fleshy piston, a kind of shifting in her mind. Then the creatures. Made of black matchsticks, or so they appeared—all jutting legs and arms and other things. And while she watched them seep into the room, the different-flavoured presence sank shadows into her head.

And then another change, a snapping into place, and she realised the client wanted her to leave. The dirty, ugly client, and she was rude to him and hid the smug satisfaction that he'd paid more than he intended; among the five-Mark bills she found a fifty.

Fool, she thinks, smirking at the memory, but immediately wonders if that was really her thought. She pauses, looks at the river and its patchy shroud of petals. The twisting, unclear thing in her mind sends shivers through her thin body. It lurks among her memories like steam curling into yellow cloud.

She stands utterly still. What is it? How did it get there? A scream threatens in the back of her mouth but she forces it back, determined not to attract attention. Policemen hang around Riverside, waiting for any excuse to apprehend a young woman for disturbing the peace.

I'll make a deal with you.

A cry escapes her lips, quickly stifled by pressing her hand over her mouth. Desperate to get inside, where she can have some privacy, she starts walking again.

She can sense the presence waiting patiently as she hurries through twisting alleyways, giving feline dens a wide berth, until she reaches a narrow staircase cut through tall buildings like a slice in the middle of a slab of grimy butter. Cool bricks brush her shoulders; discarded papers and other, less pleasant waste rustles and squelches beneath her thin shoes. She passes a heap of scrap metal, once a living construct but eroded too far now to be more than junk. Someone has already claimed an arm and a foot. The disorderly remains of limbs and other pieces remind her of the matchstick creatures, and she wonders if they are related to constructs. *No. They are something altogether different*

Gulping back a scream-gasp of fear, she hurries upwards.

Near the top of the stairs she pushes open a splinter-board door with two new bullet holes, steps over a putrefying corpse and runs along the corridor to her door at the end. The key on a chain around her ankle opens it, and she ducks inside.

A small window with half a pane of glass admits pale yellow light, casting the lithographs of famous concubines on her walls in an unnatural glow. She tosses her jacket onto the rail running along one wall and drops onto her mattress. The red cushions and green blanket offer only a frail imitation of their usual comfort.

She doesn't have to wait long. With what she would term a smile, if the thing possessed the physical parts for it, the presence stirs again.

I'll make a deal with you.

"I don't understand." Panic seeps into her voice.

I will only be here for a short time. You need not fear me.

Gripping her knees tighter to her chest, she whispers, "Please, I don't understand. What's happening?"

The answer to that question is exactly what I seek to unfold.

She shakes, waiting for it to continue.

The lifting has stalled.

"Oh." The weight of her one-word reply grows in the silence that stretches afterwards.

Without the lifting, Retyelnen will be consumed, devoured in a saraq-feast.

There are shades here that I need to_understand better before I present my report and the lifting can resume, if indeed it will.

"Who . . . " Speech dries on her tongue. She realises she's thirsty and kneels up, reaching for the basin beside her bed. The water is brown and smells but it moistens her throat well enough. "Who's your report for?"

The constructs only agreed to lift the city because we believed it in the best interests of all. Now the under-city creatures suggest this is not so. It pauses, deciding what to say next. You need to go to Minister Rulbunn. He has been known to conduct private meetings in his bedroom with whores present.

Orgy and business all in one, how convenient, thinks the wry part of Mari's mind. But apprehension quickly tramples humour. Rulbunn has a reputation. "He only likes part-construct girls," she says. "I'm all flesh. And I'm not putting metal anywhere on my body, 'specially not those places."

Not all of his colleagues and associates share his tastes. You will be welcomed by them, I'm sure.

"Right." It's easier to think of this as just another business arrangement. She understands that, at least. "Their names?"

Π

You are ready, you are willing. You are a step, a shortcut. But you are also an experience, one of many hoarded like precious packets in my clockwork vaults. With you I gain another slant on human life, and for that you are far more than just a conduit.

Π

Fighting back what feels like a steamfly brawl in her gut, Mari pushes a lock of sunset hair behind one ear and knocks on the iron door with her other hand. A strip of metal slides away, revealing a pair of dark eyes. "Name?" barks a dislocated voice.

"Mariko Illenta."

The strip slides back and, moments later, the door creaks open. She slips through the small gap and finds herself pressed against a wall by the dark eyes' owner. Panic flits through her but she holds still. This isn't the first time she's faced intimidation.

"You don't spread what you hear, little girl, or I cut you." The brute wiggles fingers that end in razor blades. "Private business is private."

She nods mutely. Of course she knows that they don't really discuss private business, that they want their carefully chosen words to seep into the city, but she suggests nothing of the sort.

"Go."

The razor blades gesture up a flight of stairs. At the top she finds a far less intimidating man who opens a wooden door, revealing a lavish room: rich red walls with shadowy cityscapes mounted at wide intervals, pieces of dark wooden furniture against the walls and, the centrepiece, a vast poster bed that she can only describe as orgy-sized. Three men lie on it, talking casually while four girls pleasure them. With a twitch of disgust, she notices two of the girls possess mechanical organs in place of the flesh most men desire.

"Miss Mariko." One of the men— she recognises him as the Minister's assistant, Josei—pushes himself up onto one elbow and smiles pleasantly. "Many thanks for coming. You look wonderful. Please, join us." With a curl of his wrist, he beckons her onto the bed.

She drops her jacket onto the floor to reveal the minimalist dress beneath. Josei smiles approvingly, and she in turn appreciates the lack of lechery in his expression. Pure aesthetic appreciation, she thinks, and has to suppress a blush. She's flattered.

She crosses to the bed and slides onto the silk sheets. As she meets Josei's lips with hers and inclines her waist so that he will run his hands over it, she wonders what the presence expects from her. What will she learn from this propaganda orgy?

You need not concern yourself with that.

For a while she follows the presence's command, loses herself in the needs of her job, but at a lull she finds her gaze wandering to Minister Rulbunn and, once again, wonders what she's supposed to be doing.

You are an experience, don't stop, don't pause, lose yourself . . .

It sounds heady, drunk almost. "Don't forget my side of the deal," she mouths. No response comes. Then she notices the matchstick figures sliding into the corner of her awareness.

They are here.

Crunching, grating—chrrkkk you called us chrrkkk—they approach the bed.

"Yes." Rulbunn sits up, easing aside one girl whose mechanical parts chatter in fear. The Minister, stocky and pale, manages to look business-like despite his nudity. Without difficulty Mari can imagine him behind a desk, dealing with any serious official situation.

The matchstick things draw closer, pulling shadows with them.

"The lifting will go ahead,"

Rulbunn says. "We will not allow your demands to threaten our safety."

Shadows darken—chrrkkk how dare you, you promised you would not abandon us, you <u>need</u> us chrrkkk—and tug back again.

"We do not need anyone but ourselves and our ingenuity. You cannot scare me, under-city creatures. You have no hold here. Be gone."

A series of insubstantial noises ripple through the air before the creatures slide away again, out of awareness.

It is not over yet, the presence muses.

The bed-play resumes as if nothing untoward has taken place. Mari lets her body work while her mind struggles to comprehend the previous minutes. Much has not been said.

Any question of witnessing further scenes is answered the moment her body next slides against Rulbunn's. His hand is smoothing over her back and rising around to her breasts when he goes lax; he slides back in the bed with a blank look on his narrow face. A faint chill shivers over Mari and she feels something slip away from her mind, and as the Minister mutters fitfully, "A deal? What is this?" she realises what has happened.

The inside of her head is solely hers once more.

She has been used.

Π

You are a new mind. Cunning and ambitious. With you I shall learn what happens to this grand city of humans. I wonder, what would you do if my kind do not consent? What would you do without your constructs?

Π

Being used is her job—she's used daily when fortune favours her, and more than daily when fortune really loves her, and she stopped herself minding years ago—but this time she feels uncomfortable. The presence kept its end of the bargain by leaving her unharmed after its departure, after it stepped off the bridge-that-was-her.

It's over.

She was granted a brief window into a world apart from her own, and she already misses it.

Frowning, she plays with a cushion and stares through her half-pane at the city. A firebird hovers over the river, searching for prey it probably won't find, and beyond its glowing form she picks out the vast, paused constructs on the yellowed horizon. The firebird is a precursor of the saraq-plants, but for the first time she wonders if it's such a bad omen. If the saraq claim the city, will matters be as straightforward as the government's dire predictions insist? She doesn't know any more.

But she is thinking about it, and about how to learn more.

The End

Beta Child, Gamma Child

by
Malon Edwards

The days he has breasts she's Annabelle Blue. The days she has a penis he's So Black He Blue.

He came upon her bathing in one corner of her bedroom, naked to the waist, bent over a basin.

Her curved back, ridged delicately by her spine, softened her angular shoulder blades; her tousled, dark hair was pinned up and exposed her long, fluted neck; her pale skin was unblemished. The hem of her striped, sun-faded dress fell to her ankles; at her feet was a ceramic pitcher glazed with lilies.

The basin, crowded atop a wooden stand flush against the wall of the master bath, shared space with two small, unmarked bottles of toilet water: one straight and tall, and the other squat and bulbous.

"I ain't gon rape you."

Whirling, she squealed a girlish but startled *Oh!*, then pressed slender arms flat against her small breasts, her cornflower blue eyes wide.

"Please doan make me leeb, miss. I so hongry an' ti'red I cain't walk no mo'."

He was fine featured with deep-set eyes framed by long, dark lashes, exquisite cheekbones, a well-formed jaw line, sensuous African thick lips and an African wide nose flared majestic. Crowned with tight, straight cornrows and dressed in too large mud-splattered denim overalls, an unbuttoned red flannel shirt and a clean white ribbed tank top which contrasted his smooth, jet-black skin, he was the most beautiful man Rebecca Livingston had ever seen.

"I jess wan to git me a bit o' food, ketch me a bit o' sleep, an' den I be on mah way."

Without taking her eyes from him, she wriggled into the top half of her dress but didn't attempt to button up the back.

"Mr. Briggs will be here shortly. I suggest you leave before he arrives."

"You a-scurred o' me, ain't you?"

He took a step forward. She took a step back.

"I ain't gon' hutt you, miss. I been walkin' all night, see, an' I's ti-red an' hongry. I jess need some food an' a place to sleep 'way from t' sun an' t' bugs, an' den I be on mah way."

Even barefoot she was a head taller than him, but she was certain he was strong enough to pin her wrists together and force her thighs apart if she tried to push past him through the doorway to escape the bedroom.

She lifted her chin and set her small mouth.

"One more step and I will, with God-given strength, rip off your testicles."

He grinned, lop-sided and wolfish.

"Mah name Blue. What's yo' name?"

"I refuse to reveal my name to an obvious criminal and soon-to-be rapist and murderer who refers to himself as 'Blue'."

"Dey calls me Blue cuz I so dark I's blue-black."

"*They*? Who are *they*? I'm sure no one from around here."

"I ain't from 'round hurr, Ms. Briggs."

"Of course you aren't. That's what I'm implying. And my name is not Ms. Briggs; it's Rebecca."

Blue held out a delicate, well-manicured hand and grinned wider.

"Please to mitt you, Miss Becca."

She crossed her arms over her slight breasts, her small mouth twisted to one side in annoyance for revealing her name to him.

"I'm sure you are."

Blue raised both hands, long slender fingers spread wide.

"I tole you I ain't gon' hurt you. 'Sides, I's too ti-red to be finkin' 'bout some poontang. Alls I can fink 'bout rit now is sumftin' to put in mah belly."

Eyes narrowed, she frowned.

"Must you be so crass?"

"I ain't so sho what dat word mean, Miss Becca."

"Crass means indelicate."

Blue said nothing, his high cheekbones slack with ignorance.

"Boorish. Rude. Impolite."

He ducked his head and rubbed the back of his neck.

"I's sorry fo' bein' impolite, Miss Becca."

He took a step closer.

"I jess want you to sho' you dat I ain't hurr to rape you."

"There are more horrible things that can befall a woman than rape."

Blue sucked his teeth and scowled, but Rebecca thought his face still looked pretty.

"Miss Becca, I cain't 'member t' last time I ate sumftin'. Jess gib me a bit o' cornpone, oah some rice an' black-eyed peas, an' den I be on mah way."

"The sheriff will eventually catch you for whatever it is you've done."

"Who say I's runnin' from t' shurrf?"

"And he and his men will most likely kill you."

Blue smiled at Rebecca in a way a man hadn't smiled at her in a long time, and she wanted to do nothing more but run downstairs and spread out before him on her dining room table a breakfast of blueberry pancakes dripping with homemade maple syrup, buttered and sugared grits, bacon, scrambled eggs with cheese, sausage links, smoked ham and toast spread with orange marmalade.

"I gots to die some time."

Smirking, he dropped his head somewhat and peered up at Rebecca through his long, dark lashes. Her calves twitched in anticipation. So to prevent her muscles from betrayal--her legs were ready to bolt down the spiral staircase for the kitchen--Rebecca dug her toes into the dark, smooth one hundred year old hardwood floor and hoped for any sort of purchase to keep her rooted to the spot.

"If you truly wanted to die, you wouldn't be running, now would you?"

"Or maybe I's runnin' cuz I doan wan' to kill nobody."

In six long strides, Rebecca crossed the distance between the washstand and the doorway where Blue hovered and her nostrils flared on their own accord with the blush-inducing tang of his musk. She did not move nor say anything for as long as she could endure, until the silence forced her to turn her back to him and say:

"Button me."

Blue did as he was told with quick, deft fingers.

"I am the teacher at the schoolhouse down the road, and I must leave soon if I am to open the doors before my pupils that need extra help arrive. You may prepare and eat whatever food there is in the icebox. You may also sleep in my bed."

Rebecca turned and faced Blue again.

"If you do not wish to be found out, then do not make any loud noises for the next two hours or so. I pay Mr. Briggs to tend the land and take care of my livestock. As long as you stay within the house and away from the windows, you won't be discovered. Mr. Briggs would not think to cross my threshold and enter my home."

Rebecca paused and breathed in once--deliberate, slow and deep.

"School lets out early afternoon. When I return, I expect you to be gone."

II

Now Miss Nora gon' tell you how things really is.

And just so y'all know, I usually don't go 'round tellin' other people's business to anybody and everybody. But this gal's business needs to be told, and by somebody who can tell it better. That other narrator who been tellin' it to you so far is dry as two-week old white bread. 'Sides, y'all need to know what's really goin' on with this gal and this boy, 'specially if y'all want to understand what happens 'tween them later.

So, let me get on with it.

Truth be told, that gal Rebecca hoped that boy Blue would still be in her house and undiscovered by Mr. Briggs when she was done teachin' them babies how to read and write and do arithmetic.

And while we tellin' the truth to shame the devil, as my momma used to say, what that gal really wanted was that boy sprawled across her bed, sleepin' soundly and tangled in her sheets, scentin' them with his man-musk, that blue-black skin of his glistenin' all wet and sexy with a light sweat from the hot summer day. But gals like Rebecca ain't 'posed to have thoughts like that.

What I mean when I say gals like Rebecca? Y'all know what I mean. Them gals who claim to be all chaste and godly and virginal. And for the most part, they are. They go to church on Sundays, Bible study on Wednesdays, and never find themselves alone in the company of an unmarried man without an old Mother Sister like me standin' next to them.

Gals like that talk the talk, but they don't always walk the walk. They get on they knees by the side of they bed every night and pray one thing to the Lord God Jesus Christ Hisself, but then dream other things the moment they lay they head on that pillow. What other things, you ask? Carnal things a little old lady like me shouldn't even be thinkin' about, let alone discussin' out in the open where everybody can hear them.

And between you, me and the lamp post, it was these same things that made a nice li'l flutter of goodness spread from that gal's stomach into her loins when she thought about the possibility of that boy's dark skin on her bone-colored sheets.

That gal couldn't stop thinkin' about that boy. She thought about him as she climbed into her bright yellow 1954 F-100 Ford pickup and gave her usual mornin' greetin's to Mr. Briggs as he rounded up her horses. She thought 'bout him as she drove the five miles to the schoolhouse down that dusty road. And she thought 'bout him as she taught them babies how to read See Spot run.

But Rebecca didn't reserve her carnal thoughts for that boy alone. When done with another day of teachin', that gal couldn't even look Mr. Briggs in his handsome, rugged tanned face and offer him a nice, tall cool glass of fresh-squeezed lemonade after lettin' the dust settle back on the road and climbin' out of that shiny new truck of hers, 'cause all she could think about was his cowboy hat hangin' on her oak headboard and his worn cowboy boots sittin' at the foot of her bed as he drawled a thank you, ma'am on her mussed up sheets.

Can't fault her for having thoughts like that, though. We all have sinned in the eyes of God, and we all fall short of the glory of the Lord. But that gal should know it ain't safe for a pretty twenty-five year old schoolmistress to be livin' all by herself on a ranch in the middle of Montana, even if she got a man to come 'round and help out with the land everyday. That's just askin' for trouble because men be havin' them same carnal feelin's, too. Even if one of these men ain't a real man.

Y'all see what I mean soon enough.

Π

When she returned, he was tangled within her duvet, fast asleep.

Her narrow nostrils widened with his scent--earth, trees, sweat and rain--the way a fugitive running through the forests and mountains of Montana during summer should smell. Underneath, his pheromones were working hard, but still she resisted the urge to slip into bed with him and went to the washstand and splashed the road dust from her face and neck.

"So, what is a black girl pretending to be white doing living alone on a ranch in the middle of the mountains?"

She started and the bottles of toilet water smashed at her feet, shards of glass skittering across the hardwood floor.

"Now, don't go all skittish with me again. I thought we were just starting to like each other."

Rebecca clutched the glazed pitcher in her left hand.

"You tricked me."

Blue sat up in bed and tucked the duvet beneath his armpits.

"Would you really have let me eat your food and sleep in your bed if I hadn't come in here with my 'Lawdy, Lawdy, I's a-runnin' fo' freedom!' routine?"

Blue rolled his eyes and wrung his hands for added effect.

"Wouldn't you have been more suspicious of me if I'd broken in here with your perfect diction and refined sensibilities? And while I apologize for the harmless deception, you and I both know I wouldn't have been able to get close to you without that dumb nigger routine."

Glass crunched beneath Rebecca's bare feet and she cried out, more so in surprise than pain. Blue moved to help her and she raised the glazed pitcher again.

"Don't. Stay over there."

"I told you I wouldn't hurt you."

She watched him, waiting three heartbeats--defiant, wary, and fierce--then placed the pitcher on the washstand, limped across the room to her backless vanity stool, removed tweezers from a drawer, and, turning away from Blue, hitched her dress to her knees.

"And I told you I didn't want you here when I returned."

"If you really meant that you would have run down the road to get that handsome cowboy of yours instead of standing there watching me sleep."

"You were pretending."

"And if anyone would know about pretending, it would be you."

Rebecca put the sleek outer edge of her arched foot on the vanity, bent forward and studied her heel, tweezers poised.

"I don't know what you're talking about."

"Do you think Mr. Briggs will still love you after he finds out you're black?"

Prying a sliver of glass from her heel, Rebecca discarded it in a waste bin next to her vanity then lifted hard eyes at Blue again.

"My mother was born and raised in Leipzig--that's in Germany--and lived there until she was twenty-eight years old and met my father. He, admittedly, is an ethnic mutt and many generations removed from Europe, but he, assuredly, is not a Negro."

"You know, it doesn't matter one bit if you wear the floppiest sun hats in your closet or order the biggest parasols from New York. The skin behind your ears doesn't lie."

"That's an old wives' tale dried up, wrinkled, pathetic, bitter and jealous Negro women from the Deep South tell."

"All it takes is one drop."

"Why are you still here? You've had some food, you've had your rest--what else do you want from me?"

"You don't remember anything at all? Not even what you did to your father?"

Rebecca opened a jewelry box on her vanity, removed a silver seven-inch letter opener fashioned to resemble a miniature sword, and clutched it so that her forearm corded.

"Before God, I swear I will kill you if you do not leave my land."

Blue scowled, but the soft lines on his face helped him retain his prettiness.

"And I if I fail to do so, I will make sure to castrate you before you violate me."

Blue threw aside the duvet and stood, careful of where he placed his small feet.

"Do I need to drop my overalls to convince you I'm not here to rape you?"

"You've been warned."

Blue unlatched his overalls at the shoulders and removed his flannel shirt and ribbed white tank top, revealing a chest perfect for draping the haute couture of Paris, Milan and Tokyo. Pausing for effect, he then slid the overalls down past his slim hips, further revealing a pair of simple white cotton panties.

"And so you don't think I'm just some confused, transgender he/she…"

Closing his eyes, Blue took a deep breath, and filled his lungs with air. As she exhaled, her sinewy pectorals rounded with sudden shape into slight breasts tipped by longer, darker nipples. Opening her eyes, she removed her panties, and as she did so her hips, buttocks, thighs and calves swelled girlish.

"Not that I expect you to do this, but if you look closely you would see that I still have a penis. It's just masquerading as a clitoris at the moment."

Rebecca placed the letter opener on the vanity, and, careful of glass shards, tiptoed her way to the walk-in closet.

"Those are horrid panties. No woman with an iota of fashion sense would allow herself to be seen wearing those."

Π

I know y'all want to hear some more 'bout that boy that ain't really a boy, but that ain't my story to tell. I'll let that other narrator tell it to y'all drier than the skin on the back end of a copper miner in Butte, Montana. What I'm here to do is tell y'all how that gal Rebecca found herself in the middle of the mountains out West in the year 1955.

Nine months ago, Rebecca, then known as Amber Braune-Jones, went to the Dictionary Man--he's the best information broker in the city-state of Chicago for y'all that don't recognize the name--and bought the identity Sally White from him. She did this 'cause the Institute of Psionics told the Department of Homeland Security to classify her as a code red rogue empath so local law enforcement could help capture her as an enemy of the State and high level terror threat for what she did to them two police officers.

Before I go on, I just want y'all to know I ain't gon tell all that gal's business. And even if I could, I don't know all that gal's business, 'specially when it comes to her and the Institute. All I know 'bout that place is them doctors and scientists that set it up over there in Hyde Park call Rebecca a gamma child. That don't make much sense to me neither right now, but I reckon y'all will understand what really that mean just like I do once that other narrator get done tellin' it.

Now, where was I? Right, that gal was named enemy of the State. How she found out 'bout that, I ain't all that certain since a paranoid empath ain't the most reliable person in the world. Anyway, to throw off the Homeland Security agents lookin' for her, Rebecca went to the best black surge between here and New Orleans--Fabien Desjardins--to have her skin whitened, her nose, lips and cheekbones de-Africanized, and her scalp quick-seed grafted with blonde hair.

And I know y'all ain't ask me, but I'm gon tell it like it is: that gal never did like them physical features her beautiful black daddy passed on to her. Even if she didn't have nobody after her, Rebecca still would have went to a black surge and got all that stuff done to herself.

But I reckon since I ain't the one bein' chased all over the country by the government, it ain't my place to say what that gal should or should not have done to herself. So that's all you gon hear from me 'bout that.

Anyway, six months ago that gal made every blood vessel in the brains of two white Arlington Heights police officers explode durin' a routine traffic stop. She did this 'cause they were beatin' to death the boy sittin' next to her in the driver's seat for bein' black, and not for sellin' her the black market cornflower blue eyes in her head right now.

Okay, so I lied. I do have more to say 'bout that.

That gal didn't have to make herself white. She had less extreme surgery options available to her. She could have darkened and straightened that curly-curly light brown hair of hers. She could have changed the shape of her eyes, or firmed her jaw, or rounded her chin. Fabien would have been able to do all that for her and more in less than an hour. It's a shame that gal turned her back on her heritage like that.

But I blame her daddy. After losing his arm in them Food Riots while stationed in Europe, he wasn't the same man. He didn't love hisself no more. H didn't love his wife and daughter no more, either. Life for him had been reduced to nothin' but anger and rage and pain, so he drank and beat his wife 'cause he didn't know how else to deal with his problems.

The thing is, he justified those beatin's. When that gal asked her daddy straight out why he backhanded her momma every other night, he told her it was 'cause her momma was white and the only reason he could live in the northwest suburbs without a permit.

So, one night after her daddy split her momma's lip and closed one of her momma's eyes, that gal made his brain explode, too.

Puttin' it like that make it sound like she did it on purpose, which she didn't. Just like she didn't set out to kill them police officers. As a gamma child, that gal's latent empathic abilities had been buried deep and didn't rise up out her subconscious 'til a few months ago.

The government knew this though, since they was the ones who made her that way. They had just been sittin' back, waitin' for somethin' like this to happen so they could go and get that gal. And namin' her enemy of the State made it that much easier for them to arrest her.

See, y'all got me tellin' all her business again. I'm 'posed to be just tellin' y'all how she got to the middle of Montana in the year 1955.

Three months ago, Sally White, then known as Rebecca Livingston, moved from Illinois to western Montana. She did this 'cause ever since she was a little girl she wanted to be an I-am-woman-hear-me-roar schoolmarm who lived alone in the mountains on a ranch tended by a handsome cowboy.

She also did this 'cause that powerful empathic mind of hers figgered government men would be knockin' on her door for what she did to them policemen. So, to hide from them, her mind created a pocket universe within a fifty-mile radius of a two-thousand acre ranch in Dillon, Montana, staffed it with a cowboy named Mr. Briggs, made the year 1955 and forced the three hundred or so residents in the area to believe the same until it could figger out what to do next. All without makin' this known to her on a conscious level.

Now I'm gon go sit down some-where so that other narrator can tell the rest of that gal's business. And Blue's, too.

II

Established half a century ago by the Collegium--a group of in-residence biologists, neurologists and psychologists at the University of Chicago--the Institute of Psionics had but one goal: to increase the average brain capacity of its students tenfold by the year 2085.

In just ten years the Collegium achieved this goal, using two main strategies: high-quality, innovative education at the

Institute of Psionics, the K-12 private school they established in the Hyde Park neighborhood, and drugs.

Under the auspices of the Collegium, the drugs were provided by researchers at the Great Lakes Naval Hospital to sixty women two months pregnant in the form of an experimental prenatal supplement for the duration of their pregnancies.

Seventy-two hours into the study, twenty women miscarried. The researchers labeled these women and their dead fetuses alpha group. Five months into the study, twenty women bore pre-term children. The researchers labeled these women and their children beta group. Seven months into the study, the remaining twenty women had uneventful births. The researchers labeled these women and their children gamma group.

Annabelle Blue, colorfully known sometimes as So Black He Blue--no pun intended--had been a beta child, and, even in the early years of her life, was an adept biopath.

At the age of three, her mother had to tame her hair into neat and even cornrows because her plump, bauble-encrusted braids were unruly and violent as they flailed about, curious and inquisitive of their surroundings.

At the age of seven, Annabelle Blue could change her eye color at will and replace missing baby teeth overnight.

And at the age of twelve, she could thicken her hips and round out her breasts and booty so the baby tees and cutoff shorts she wore in summer clung tight and turned the heads of both boys and men.

Dismayed and disturbed by her daughter's increased body control proficiency, including an unnatural manipulation of tissue and organs at the cellular level and a burgeoning ability to regulate her pheromones and hormones, Isabelle Blue returned to the Great Lakes Naval Hospital with daughter Annabelle Blue, where, after a four-hour consultation and evaluation, the researchers enrolled her as a student at the Institute of Psionics.

Staffed by junior members of the Collegium, the Institute of Psionics--affectionately called the Institute by both professors and students and herein referred to as such--offered accelerated courses and unorthodox classroom instruction to all grade levels by way of small group settings and one-on-one tutorials as a way to maximize students' skills, abilities and potential.

While the early success of the Institute could be attributed to various factors, most noted was the professor-to-student ratio: 10:1. Such a small and intimate classroom setting allowed gamma child Amber Braune-Jones--also known as Sally White, also known as Rebecca Livingston--to flourish and excel as the most powerful empath engineered by the Collegium, even if her mental abilities were latent.

As with all gamma children, Amber Braune-Jones's mental abilities manifested during her twenties. And like the other gamma children, her abilities had been triggered by a traumatic event.

However, unlike the other gamma children, the emergence of her empathic ability to diffuse the negative emotions of others in her vicinity with abrupt and violent finality was caused by the exceptional brutal beating her drunken father had given her mother the night Amber Braune-Jones had been packing to move into her just acquired condominium a week after graduating from Northwestern University.

In a more dissimilar vein, beta children often exhibited some sort of manifestation of their abilities during early childhood--case in point, Annabelle Blue--but did not have full access to these abilities until beta maturation was complete, which could take years.

For example, while Annabelle Blue could, with varying success, control her free-hanging braids when she was three years old, she could not generate an entire tooth overnight until she was seven years old.

And while she had full control of her female secondary sex characteristics when she was twelve years old, including manipulation of her subcutaneous fat, she did not exhibit even a modicum of control over her male secondary sex characteristics until she was sixteen years old--an unfortunate and embarrassing incident that took place six summers ago.

Despite their brain capacity and diverse abilities, beta children and gamma children were quite normal at times. So, it was not surprising in the least that, at the age of sixteen, Annabelle Blue developed a profound and overwhelming crush on a boy who also attended the Institute.

Just as well, it should not be surprising that, one day Annabelle Blue and said boy, gamma child Billy Patterson, decided to go to his house after their Biomolecular Chemistry class because his parents weren't home and he lived in Hyde Park, just blocks from the Institute.

However, what very much surprised them both was the seven inch erect penis Annabelle Blue grew with sudden swiftness from her clitoris as the two kissed and fondled naked on Billy Patterson's bed.

At first, Billy Patterson hadn't seemed to mind her penis. Eyes closed with Annabelle Blue on top of him, her fingers entangled in his short, boyish blond curls and his aroused penis wedged into her labia, Billy Patterson had reached down to adjust himself for penetration--and grasped Annabelle Blue's penis instead.

Unperturbed--at least initially--Billy Patterson continued to kiss Annabelle Blue with a heavy and clumsy tongue, while applying consistent and intense stimulation upon her new penis. But soon his grip upon the member became painful as he pulled and yanked her.

That night, while crying herself to sleep in her own bed, Annabelle Blue wondered what she could have done to bring about a different outcome, and concluded Billy Patterson's actions had been driven by homophobia.

Yet six years later, when the incident crossed her brow in an idle moment of remembrance as it did at some point

everyday since, she was not so sure anymore homophobia had been the absolute reason for Billy Patterson's reaction. His inexperience when it came to sex, his general shy and introverted nature, and her then-incompetence with the manipulation of her hormones and pheromones all had contributed to what happened.

Though, these days during her most lucid moments just before slumber, Annabelle Blue blames the incident on the higher than normal levels of androstadienone in her saliva.

A hormone typically known to increase a woman's sexual arousal when in the saliva of men, Annabelle Blue believes androstadienone had the exact opposite effect on Billy Patterson when she kissed him.

However, during her most sober moments, she also believes he had been embarrassed and disgusted by another glans, lubricated with pre-ejaculate, rubbing against his own, arousing him to no end.

Nevertheless, her reasoning could not change how the events transpired: Billy Patterson wrenching Annabelle Blue's penis with savage and violent twists; Annabelle Blue chiseling her facial features masculine, shedding seventeen percent body fat, and then doubling her size and muscle mass in mere seconds in order to pummel him bloody and comatose.

This, of course, did not sit well with Billy Patterson's parents. Nor did it sit well with the detractors and critics of the Institute.

From its inception, the Institute had garnered nothing but negativity from the general public. If the editorial board at the Sun Times wasn't attacking it for being exclusory and not accepting children with an I.Q. below 120, Yellow Jacket Jane and the Coalition Of Modified Beings excoriated it for being discriminatory and having but one modified student among the one-hundred and thirty total enrolled.

So, when Annabelle Blue beat Billy Patterson half to death, the Institute, forthwith and straightaway, removed her from the school and placed her in the care of the federal government. It was the most viable option for her considering the close relationship the Institute had with the Department of Homeland Security.

The Collegium, as an autonomous entity with considerable clout and power within Chicago, did not extend its influence very far beyond the borders of the city-state. That did not mean the Collegium was an unknown entity outside Chicago, though. With its ties to the Naval Hospital, the State Department and the Department of Homeland Security were well aware of its numerous projects, including the Institute.

The Department of Homeland Security was so aware that they created a recruitment pipeline within the Institute to train beta children post-graduation as agents for their various campaigns, missions and operations throughout the world.

Once recruited, Annabelle Blue's first task had been to spy upon and infiltrate the group of rogue gamma children headquartered in the John Hancock Building. Led by the Hanged Man, they used their latency as insurgence against the city-state. However, once Amber-Braune-Jones became gamma mature, Annabelle Blue's mole assignment was put on hold and she was ordered to neutralize and capture Amber Braune-Jones instead.

Aside from Billy Patterson, Annabelle Blue hadn't incapacitated nor neutralized another person. And while she had been successful with Billy Patterson (he still lay in a comatose state), Annabelle Blue hoped her encounter with Amber Braune-Jones would not end the same.

Which, it did not. But the climax of the encounter was not quite what Annabelle Blue expected, to say the least, as you shall soon discover, dear reader.

II

Rebecca removed two pairs of panties from the cherry wood wardrobe in her walk-in closet.

"Pink would look lovely on you. But so would baby blue."

She held each pair in turn against Annabelle Blue's waist.

"Which do you think?"

"The blue pair."

Rebecca smiled, her cheeks schoolgirl pink.

"Of course. Try them on."

Annabelle Blue frowned, hesitant and unsure.

"I just became shy all of a sudden."

She slipped on her white tank top, dark nipples erect beneath.

"I can leave the room if you wish."

Rebecca placed the panties on the bed and paused before moving towards the door.

"No, it's fine. Stay."

"Are you certain?"

"Yes."

"Would you like me to turn my back?"

"No. Just close your eyes."

Rebecca cast her eyes downward and bowed her head, as if offering up prayer.

"You may open them."

She opened her eyes and saw Annabelle Blue arms akimbo, unsure how to pose, her back stooped with inelegance.

"Beautiful. There is no better shade against your skin."

"You're just being polite."

"No, it's true. Come here to the mirror."

Examining herself from the side in the full-length Cheval mirror complete with beveled edges, Annabelle Blue arched her back to accentuate her buttocks.

"I am not sure if I've ever worn a more comfortable pair of underwear."

Rebecca's cornflower blue eyes flitted over Annabelle Blue's breasts, mons pubis, hips, and again, breasts.

"You need a bra."

She returned to the closet and Annabelle Blue could hear the wardrobe drawers squeal as Rebecca searched.

"I must get Mr. Briggs to oil these."

The racks of sun dresses, wide-brimmed hats, and colorful parasols from New York muffled her voice.

"Don't trouble yourself; I have little need for support now."

Rebecca poked her head out in time to glimpse the last stages of Annabelle Blue's transformation: her jaw elongated into a thick right angle; her breasts flattened into curved, sinewy pectorals; her panties strained to contain the breadth and length of his now erect penis.

"Oh my."

In two strides he was at the entrance of the closet and clutching Rebecca's straight blonde hair in one knurled, blue-black hand.

"You promised you wouldn't hurt me."

Blue pulled his panties down to just beneath his buttocks with his free hand and smiled as he rammed Rebecca's face into his crotch with his other, bruising her thin lips and slender nose against his penis.

"Trust me; this won't hurt."

Lubricated with Rebecca's saliva and swift tears, Blue used his penis to pry apart her teeth, ignoring the loss of skin and the abrasion of flesh by bone. Then tightening his buttocks and constricting his sphincter, ultimately seeking the soft, wet flesh of Rebecca's tongue, Blue thrust once, felt the textured warmth of her taste buds, felt his glans strike her soft palate and uvula, heard her gag—

—and screamed as he deconstructed within the silent explosion of white.

II

Now, don't get me wrong when I say that boy who ain't really a boy ain't got no common sense at all. We all know he got some cleverness about him 'cause if he didn't he wouldn't have pulled off such a ruse on that gal like he did.

I ain't sayin' that boy a mastermind, but he didn't just wake up one mornin' and tell hisself, 'I think I'm gon pretend to be a Jim Crow buck runnin' from the shurrf to get in the good graces of that gal who killed her daddy and two policemen then went to Montana and made everything and everyone in a fifty-mile radius 'round her the 1950s.' A person got to plot and plan real good with other people to do stuff so coordinated and detailed like he did.

And if that meant him mem'rizin' the ninety-six page dossier the State Department gave him on that gal to make sure he didn't mess up the ruse, then he should have done that 'cause we talkin' about life and death here. Blue knew good and well what was gon happen to him if he tried to rape that gal before neutralizin' and capturin' her. That boy knew that gal would bust out her psionic attack at the slightest bit of negativity rollin' off him.

I mean, it ain't like rape is a pleasurable experience. Don't let them Japanese people fool you. Just because they say them women in those holo sex vids they make enjoy bein' raped don't mean it's true. I may be older than both dirt and black pepper, but I ain't no fool. Them God-forsaken things they be doin' over there in Tokyo ain't about nothin' but horrible painful and 'motions. And don't try to tell me otherwise.

Look at what y'all made me do. Y'all got Miss Nora all off track again. What was I tellin' y'all about? That's right. I 'member. Blue underestimatin' that gal. That boy got too big for his britches is what he did. He got arrogant. He thought his hormones and pheromones would save him. He thought as long as he was strong enough, as long as he smelled good enough--as long as he was man enough--that gal couldn't resist him and wouldn't make his brain explode. That boy should have known good and well that was exactly what that gal was gon do to him.

But deep down inside I think that boy knew that. He knew it when him and that voice coach Homeland Security got him practiced that I's a'runnin' fo' mah freedom! accent and routine 'til all hours of the night and made it more natural than his very own inflections and mannerisms.

He knew it when that period wardrobe specialist Homeland Security got him took four and a half hours searchin' thrift stores to find that tank top, flannel shirt and overalls he was wearin' when he met that gal, and then turned 'round and took another two hours to stress the clothes just right so they looked like he been runnin' from the law through the woods for days on end.

And that boy knew it like he knew the name his momma gave her when that actin' coach Homeland Security got him said and did things to make him hot and mad on purpose, then 'minded him of his breathin' exercises and relaxation techniques right before he let his 'motions get the best of him.

Blue and his actin' coach had kept a tally of how many times he would have died to that gal's psionic attack against how many times he would have lived by keepin' his cool. I ain't got to tell y'all which side that boy ended up on, but for y'all nosey ones out there, the tally went 558 to 562. Pretty close if you ask me, but close don't really count 'cept for horse shoes and hand grenades. And that boy wasn't throwin' neither.

I can understand that boy's arrogance, though. Now, that ain't to say I agree with it, but I do understand it.

There wasn't anybody in the world more qualified and prepared to neutralize and capture that girl than that boy.

Between what the Collegium and the Institute did with him, and what Homeland Security did with him, that gal shouldn't have had no chance at all when Blue walked up them stairs and into her bedroom. And as you saw, he almost got her. But we both know what happens when we start usin' words like 'almost' and 'pretty close.'

That gal sho got a powerful mind, though. Prolly got the most powerful mind in the world. I ain't lyin'. I already told you my momma ain't raise no fool, and now I'm tellin' you she ain't raise no liar, neither. That gal was the first person to resist Blue, and he was the most powerful biopath in the world. Before her, wasn't nobody able to resist that boy's pheromones, once he mastered his control of them.

To test Blue, Homeland Security would bring in all sorts of people for him to work his mojo on--young people, old people; black people, white people; fat people, skinny people; smart people, dumb people; men, women; boys, girls--once they even brought in a monkey for that boy to ply his pheromonal wiles on. None of them could resist. Not even that monkey.

When that boy had them people in the palm of his hand on that base, animalistic level--which made that whole irreverent and sacrilegious situation with the monkey make more sense--Blue could have them people do whatever he wanted. Any suggestion that boy gave them, no matter how big or small, was a command they couldn't disobey, even if it went against they most sacred and most cherished ideals and morals.

So, when that other narrator told you that gal was annoyed with herself for revealin' her name to Blue, that was 'cause of that boy and his pheromones.

And when that other narrator told you that gal could all but contain herself from runnin' down them stairs to her kitchen and spreadin' out a breakfast for Blue she shouldn't have been spreadin' out for nobody but her husband, that was 'cause of that boy and his pheromones.

So, I ain't surprised at all at that boy's arrogance. Give a young black boy a lot of talent and a lot of power and he ain't gon turn out no way but arrogant. And it ain't his fault. We can't put all the blame on him. That's the way this city-state set up; that's the way we as black people raise our black boys.

And we also shouldn't be surprised our black boys grow up angry and stay angry. Just look at that gal's daddy. That man was so angry he killed his wife and tried to kill his only child, his baby girl. But all that anger wasn't his. Some of that anger belongs to this city-state. Some of that anger belongs to Arlington Heights. Some of that anger belongs to the Chicago Council of Guilds for the mess they allow to happen here.

I'd be angry too if I was 'minded everyday, every time I passed through the gate into Arlington Heights and showed my residence permit that the only reason they was lettin' me in was because the person I married is white.

If you ask me, and I know you didn't but I'm tellin' you anyway, that's more than enough reason to be angry.

Now, I ain't sayin' it's reason enough to kill somebody over, but her daddy had every right to be mad about that.

Still, that don't mean just because somebody is angry they have to right to act on that anger, 'specially in violence. And I'm talkin' 'bout that gal's daddy, Blue, and anybody else who get mad and then want to go hurt somebody.

But Miss Nora know Blue was mad at the world, at the Council, at the Collegium, at the Institute, at Homeland Security, at his momma, at that gal, at everyone for making his life horrible and reducin' it to hormones and pheromones and nothin' more.

Life can't be enjoyable when every minute of everyday you in a small room and somebody is always askin' you to manipulate better and faster than the last time, and you only twelve years old. That ain't a good way at all for a boy to spend his formative years.

Still, that don't excuse that boy for his actions, which bring me back to what I was tellin' y'all in the first place: that boy ain't got no common sense. Common sense should have told Blue to suppress his 'motions and not let that gal know he was angry. Common sense should have told that boy he could do whatever he pleased to that gal whenever he pleased once he had her neutralized and captured her. But common sense don't seem to win out with our young black boys these days, and that's a shame.

That boy was talented, though, and I'm sad to see him gone. But on the other side of that, I'm happy to see that gal got herself out of that strange li'l world she created out there in Montana, pulled herself together, and is on her way back here to Chicago to meet up with the Hanged Man.

Ain't no better place in the world for her but here with him. She'll be 'round a whole lot of other people just like her--people who have been ridiculed by friends and family, people who have been abused one way or another by the city-state, people with power and strength and wisdom and knowledge.

Now, I know y'all prolly sayin' the best place for that gal is back in the suburbs with her momma, 'specially when you think about what the two of them went through, but things just ain't that simple for Amber Braune-Jones right now.

Not only do she have Homeland Security on one side callin' her a terrorist and sayin' she the most dangerous homegrown threat in the country right now so she need to be captured and executed right away, she got the Council on the other side sayin' they want to do pretty much the same thing to her for murderin' her daddy and the two police officers.

But don't y'all worry none about Amber Braune-Jones. She gon be all right once she find the Hanged Man. I'm gon make sure of that myself by bein' the first to give her a nice big hug when she get here.

The End

Paint The Town

by
Anne Pinckard

He is a sad, pathetic fuck. Surely that's what everyone thinks of him, anyway, and with his hands shoved into his jeans pockets, that's precisely what he feels like. He imagines each beat of his walks spells out his fate in so many syllables: pa- the- tic- fuck. He hunches his shoulders and hustles down the gaudy, electrified strip of Akihabara to escape the relentless rhythm.

Hell, it's Tokyo, 2008. He tries to rekindle the excitement he'd dared to feel stepping off the plane. Japan! Traveling! Freedom! But now his Converse sneakers are beating out another message: too late, too late. *He's* not the exotic here. He might have been, ten, fifteen years ago, when he was pre twenty five and before the internet made oceans insignificant. Then he might have been a curio among the Japanese. Now, his Diesel jeans mean nothing. His painstakingly flattened hair, his studded belt buckle, his indy-band tee shirt, mean nothing. His piercings and tattoos mark him as a wannabe; or worse, a has-been. Even his perfect, white teeth, the result of a high school endured with various contraptions in his mouth, mean nothing. In the faces of those passing by him, blurred by the flashing lights, he sees only the cool boredom of disenchantment. The same old shit. Old shit, old shit, his feet echo.

She materializes out of the shadows, rendered aquatic by the green neon lights overhead. "Looking for a good time?" she says.

The cliched pick up line, in her accent—"rooking"—catches him off guard and he snorts in amusement—is this for real? —before he has a chance to recover his disaffection. Her smile flashes like a knife. He cannot tell her age or her intent. The light above him turns to orange, lighting her on fire. The next second it's blue, and she's a corpse. When the light turns white she draws back into the dark.

He almost continues on his way, but the challenge has been made to his self identity. This is what he came for, after all. Adventure. A new experience. Or has he come to affirm his convictions that globalization has destroyed everything, originality is extinct, and how the hell could he be so immoral as to *travel*, for fuck's sake, 7,000 miles across the world? Think of the carbon emissions! He might as well bend over and let the oil barons in!

"Hold up!" He's spoken before he's even realized what he's done. He glances over his shoulder, feeling as if he's been caught as a fraud. He jogs down the alley after her. "Connichiwa!" It's the only Japanese word he's learned.

She pauses; he falters. A cigarette trembles in her hand. Her long dark hair falls around her face like water. She is thin as a reed, swathed in white. Suddenly he's convinced he's misread her. She's not offering sex. It's a terrible mistake. And then she smiles, revealing a mouth full of crooked little teeth, but it's the gold tooth which restores his Americanness.

"You got another one of those?" he says. For conversation only. Cigarettes are available for a couple hundred yen anywhere by vending machine.

She lights one for him and hands it over. He can taste her saliva and the aromatic oil of her lipstick. He wonders if he's ingesting whale blubber, another cardinal sin, and he smiles. She leads him through the bowels of the city. Everywhere there's people —you can't get away from them here—then she ducks into a doorway where he catches up to her.

"Where are we going?" he says. "Is this your place?"

"No." The door opens to black. An urgent, primal beat thrums. Cold fingers slip around his wrist and he's pulled inside.

Hell, he could have resisted. But another clichéd thought comes to him: Follow the white rabbit. None of this, he concludes, is real. "I'm going to call you Alice," he shouts to her. He's almost disappointed to find they are climbing up real enough stairs. She opens another door, and here at last he can make out the music. It's house, with a good, pungent beat. Strobe and black lights illuminate the forms gyrating and grinding in the jungle heat. He feels something stirring within. Excitement? He dismisses the notion.

A survey of the room reveals industrial pipes and vents running along the ceiling high above. Plastic is the decoration of choice. Sheets of it hang everywhere. Ah, the opulence! The blatant waste of petro-chemicals! It makes him want to laugh. The beat surges through him and he thinks about grabbing her hips and rocking with her. He imagines their bodies pressed against each other, and wonders what her real name is.

Cheers break out around him. They're hugging her, welcoming her, and him, by association. What has he gotten himself into? She pulls him onto a stage of some kind. Here, too, there's plastic, lining the floor and hanging like curtains around them. She pushes him into the single metal folding chair in the middle. "Stay," she whispers in his ear. Entranced, he watches. She's going to do a dance for him, but here? In front of all these people? He was never much of an exhibitionist. Sure, a grope in an elevator or on the train, but this display makes his penis whimper and shrink.

She begins to sway, not quite to the

beat, but to something much more compelling, her own pulse. His own blood beat rises in his temples and throbs with her dance. Her eyes close, her head lolls back. She looks like a marionette operated by a drunken master, but the dance is more sensual, more erotic than anything he can remember.

The audience is screaming in Japanese. He can feel them pressing against him though they stand at the foot of the stage. Their body heat is stifling, keeping him in his chair; that, and the spell she's weaving with her body and with her hair, which has drawn closed around her face. A faceless body, dancing. She begins to strip, and he shivers.

Someone approaches from behind, holding a tray. Naked, she takes something from it—a straight razor. His gut runs sick. He wants to flee but he's stuck there.

She continues her rolling, disjointed dance with the open blade. In the light, she's all angles, planes, and knobs, skinnier even than he thought possible. Metal meets flesh. He flinches, wishing he could close his eyes but he can't. They've dried open or something. Thick coils of blood run down her arms. She slices again; more blood runs. He thinks he's going to be sick. Her hair parts just a bit, and she smiles. Then she's straddled him, her breasts dangling in front of his face, her blood smearing his body. She slices right through his $400 leather jacket. She makes shreds of his tee shirt. She stains his jeans with her fluids. A hundred diseases run through his mind. His heart is beating so fast now he swears it's going to explode.

Facing him, she puts the blade against her thin arm and presses. He expects horror as the blood wells from the cut and trickles onto his bare skin, but there is peace in her eyes, and something . . . Life? Catharsis? Ecstasy? More cliches. He doesn't know what to call it. He's never seen anything like it before. He touches her, tracing a trail of blood over her nipples and down her belly. He kisses her wrist. Grinning, she tosses her clumped hair over her shoulder and urges him to stand. He wraps his arms around her, feeling her move with him, around him, through him. Others have ascended the stage. He feels someone pressing behind him. A dick, erect, pokes at his buttocks. He laughs, and they all dance in her blood.

The End

Sweet Adult Cell

by
Ray Succre

Sweet Michelle's Michael

How she might live is Michael,
or in which manner she sees,
and where Michael would be a man, she is,
and where Michael is a woman, she lives.

One on either side of a pane,
the reflective sort,
knew the other,
twisting her balls and tapping his tits.

Both, one, and between them,
a bible blackbird squawk and damn,
a tradition, one of many.
Between these insightful condemnations,
sweet Michelle's Michael,
tied in a fiber of lore.

The Orange Cell

The red cell stretches, oblique and amorphous,
enveloping the yellow cell, digesting.

Then blossomed is a large, orange cell.
Its flagella flits it forward in curves.

You lazy god.
I splay my conceptive hole like the gates of Kiev
and ask to be fangled in juice,
but you marry.

I ingest you and we lay in a stinking tide pool,
poured by our rectums into a rocky perch pit;
the gulls drink it and the ants drink it,
but you marry.

Passing the land on our heads,
I swagger and fall, scraping my shin,
and you bend and lick the porous wound,
proposing.

We are absurd, delicious fucks.
Dangling lover,
I dress in the fashion of my day,
dumbly silked with my neck tongued numb.
You climb into my clothes like a cold.

We marry, lazy and spread open
on the large-breasted, matrimonial feast.

We are the enthralled, drinking creature
atop its kill in the sun.

Adult Content

My young, dumbly scented boys
who church in my cellar, pause-playing,
swipe their parents' remotes at ass-cracks.

They're learning to aim for the face.

Here I have hunched, halo and horns,
fucking in the rough, for the day,
for the wights who watch in rooms.

I may show the unaware look, oh my, oh no,
dilated on the slim, curved mantilla.
See? Like so.

To find me somewise alive, look to my
flush complexion, or in the aspect divined
from having the stings of bees in your heart.

There I am from the start of the world.

'Blue Hand' by Elaine Borthwick

'ai3' by Dave Migman

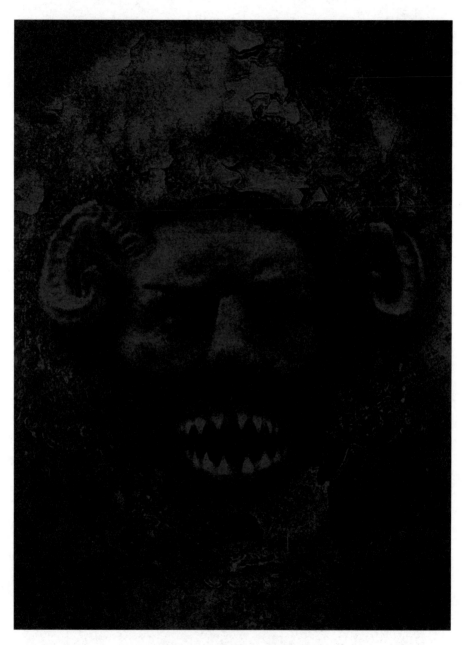

'dfcclr' by Dave Migman

'Empire' by Dave Migman

'Gal' by Dave Migman

'In the Cathedral' by Dave Migman

'Three of Clubs' by Kurt Huggins & Zelda Devon

'Three of Hearts' by Kurt Huggins & Zelda Devon

'Three of Diamonds' by Kurt Huggins & Zelda Devon

'Three of Spades' by Kurt Huggins & Zelda Devon

Top: 'Is it so bad to be banal?' by Luke Drozd
Bottom: 'Not So White' by Dave Migman

"Who Are You?' by Flavia Testa-Lytle
Pen ink collage, 2008.

'Zed' by Dave

'Summoner' by Dave Migman

'Branded' by Luke Drozd

Images by O-Ten Photography

Model: Micci Oaten

Photographer: Chris Oaten

The Beauty And The Beast

by
Micci Oaten

Pondering over what i would like to write about for this issue, I was confronted by a very swollen and bruised Maria who had just come home from a video shoot with a film company. (The film company I am not at liberty to mention as she was forced to sign a 'gagging order' to never speak of her ordeal.) When the girl you love walks into the room looking pissed off and hurt, it is something you cannot ignore.

What I could get out of her, as I am a persistent bugger, was that she was sent by one of her agencies to film a fetish shoot. There was no mention of anything Maria hadn't done before—spanking, handcuffs etc. When she got there she was confronted by two guys and a cameraman. The cameraman was running the show. The impression I got of this cameraman was that he is hen-pecked and wanted to vent his frustrations for not having enough control of his life onto an innocent party, preferably a female. If I could tell you what the film was called then you would completely understand why I have come to this impression.

The camera guy had laid out lots of tools he wanted the two guys to use on her—including an electronic dog collar with a setting up to 15 (the standard setting in the UK is up to 8). This device is banned in Wales and is being debated on now in the rest of the UK. He also had tazer, an electrical cattle prod and lots of other torturous devices.

Maria is a very headstrong lady (she can also look after herself as she does martial arts) and decided she would do the shoot but on her terms. If she hadn't been so strong then what could have happened, I shudder to imagine.

Even so, she still came home with a swollen lower back injury, a bruised collar bone and lots of marks. Can you imagine how infuriated I was? Let's put it this way: I have informed the necessary authorities in their area as they are using illegal devices and also do not have medical staff or insurance. It would only take a girl to have a weak heart, low blood sugar or epilepsy to seriously threaten her life with electronic devices. I truly hope this company is closed down, as this has nothing to do with sex whatsoever.

I have in the past been part of the porn industry, as a lesbian porn star, so I know how most of it works. I have worked for many reputable companies that show the girls lots of respect. I have also been put into situations that were not so pleasant. One guy (the company is based in Halifax) told me that I had a serious attitude problem because he tried to touch me and I glared at him as I moved away. He refused to film me, so a girl took his place. He seemed to think I would be impressed by the huge car parked outside and therefore would be dumb enough to take his manner with a smile. Ha!

The agencies push and push to try and get you to do stuff you wouldn't ever dream of doing by using the 'Well, you're not getting any younger' and 'If you don't then your work will dry up' crap. Some agencies also have a knack for not telling the model all the necessary details about the shoot, hence what happened to Maria. Therefore these kinds of agencies should also be held accountable if there are any problems or injuries.

I have modelled for seven years and I have been told I could carry on if I wanted to. It's your look and your presence that attracts people to your pictures. For the past five years, Chris has taken my photos as I became sick of creepy old photographers who tried to touch me. They give photographers a bad name because not all photographers are like this.

I have recently done a shoot with Maria where we were photographed making love. We wanted to do this shoot to show people the difference between fake girl-on-girl and real affection. This is about to be published in *Knave Magazine* and was shot by my long term male partner, Chris, who only shoots the art—he refuses to shoot anything misleading.

You can see a selection of his photos in this issue of *Polluto* under O-Ten Photography.

Chris, along with a fellow photographer, Scottie, is setting up a film company to correct the serious flaws within the porn industry. Maybe guys who watch and believe fake standard porn will see that it has no grasp on reality whatsoever, when seeing an intelligent comparison.

I always do my research on any subject that I write about and what I have seen on the internet is not for the faint-hearted. How extreme will these companies go? Probably as far as the incoming requests, which is certainly worrying.

It also begs the question of how much people are being de-sensitised. If you compare each decade and how much people can tolerate seeing on their TV sets (and now on our computers and phones), then you can start to see that this could seriously take us all back to hitting each other over the head with flint and dragging females around by their hair. And people believe we are civilised, or is it the fact that ignorance makes us believe this?

Where will it end? It is transparent to anyone these filmmakers' next step is to be handcuffed to a prison officer, and quite rightly so.

So what is porn about? Answer: it is about watching people having sex. Fetish is part of the sexual experience with someone you truly trust to empower you and to take you to places that are very hard to describe, but which are extremely exciting and a confirmation of the bond that you have together. Fetish always has a rule that you both have safety words that have no relevance to sex, so that everyone's boundaries are respected.

Porn is a very shallow view of sex, which does concern me and should concern you too. For example, you have a son or daughter that is now becoming curious about sex and starts to ask lots of questions on what it involves doing and why. Do you give your offspring a porn movie? Nope, you probably wouldn't, but their friends may or will know how to get hold of one. What impression will he/she get? That girls (or boys) are there to be used in anyway you feel and that they are to be taught a lesson for liking sex too much? That the orgasm is for the guy only and girls must make stupid orgasm sounds to make the guy happy? How about that lesbian porn is about the girls just getting themselves ready for the man, because without the man they couldn't possibly be fulfilled?

Why does a lot of straight porn have to be derogatory towards females? What does that say about the male viewer who likes to see females being demeaned? Their mentality needs questioning. Do fathers like the thought of their own daughter being treated in the same manner they enjoy watching in a porn movie? Because this is quite often the first impression a male will have of sex and the father will know this.

Contrary to popular belief, sex is not all about the male anatomy. It's all about an intimate bonding, not some idiot who has no control or respect for the female and spurts all over her face!

What angers me the most is that a lot of porn companies are run by men who want to vent frustrations or because it's the only way they can get laid by a female since their social skills suck! Why are most of these guys ugly, old, fat fuckers who slobber and grope young girls? It makes my flesh crawl.

Do I sound like a man hater yet? I'm not. I don't want to tar all people with the same brush, but surely if you are a guy reading this, you want these guys to stop giving you a rotten reputation, don't you?

Queer as Folk, The L Word—why are these series so popular? Because they show every angle of human emotion not gynaecological detail. They have sex scenes and the scenes are a lot more like reality because when you have sex you're not seeing everything from all angles and in close detail. You're enjoying the moment, and this is what these shows express. Do you really need to see all the details to become turned on? Have you no imagination or are you just lazy?

The number of females who were turned on by Stuart in Queer as Folk was astounding and he showed no physical emotion towards a female. It didn't stop the actor receiving tons of mail from females wanting him. It was his confidence and his presence that made him very horny.

Yes, porn is just about 'getting down to the sex' and there is nothing wrong with wanting to watch that, as long as it has been filmed in a responsible manner so that it doesn't encourage sex as a tool to express aggression and frustration.

The natural expression of having sex is being stripped of its dignity by screwed up individuals who seriously need to get some help.

I have named this piece 'The Beauty and the Beast' as something so beautiful is being marred by ugliness. Maybe one day we can all make sex beautiful again.

The End

Heart Of Cement

by
Lawrence R. Dagstine

In the gay community it was what Alex Williams called a "Nothing Week"—nothing promised, nothing beckoned, nothing happened. He wound up on Friday at its end and its beginning, because it was the end of another workweek and the beginning of the weekend with a vacuum of time to fill and nothing stirring on the listless air of his Lower East Side apartment. How ironic, he thought bleakly, that the telephone—an instrument which shrilled incessantly during his workdays in telecommunications, as it demanded his voice and his presence—lay silent and dead in his home, where he ached for it to ring. Sometimes, in his restive pacing, he would stop and stare down at its inert form on the table, wondering whether its complicated insides were really coiled there underneath, ready to activate, to announce in measured trills that someone other than his mother was thinking of him, or whether it was just a disemboweled piece of metal incapable of communication.

When he stopped to think who might call, no one sprang to mind. And if he were just going to hang around moping, he would miss the outgoing tide of activity outside his window.

Finally, he got up and said: "Ah, screw this! Fresh air is better than dead air. I need to go somewhere—anywhere!—to have a drink, hear voices, look into the faces of others. I can't stay cooped up like this my entire life."

He grabbed his leather bomber from the side of the couch and his keys from the nightstand and left the apartment.

The air outside was sharp and lively, and clear for a November night. It wasn't until he was walking up Bowery Street that he acknowledged to himself he was actually going out to try and find a man. When this realization sliced through him, he had a feeling of shock—he was short, slightly scrawny, but after three years of living in the city, he was still somewhat in the closet—then, almost belligerently, he swept it aside. What's so bad about this? he asked himself. What's so terrible if I speak to some nice guy at a respectable bar and he speaks to me? For Christ's sake, this is the 21st century!

Frowning as he walked amidst the milling people, hands deep in his pockets, a dozen arguments sprang up in his mind, batting down any last minute doubts that might have lurked there. The only difference between meeting a gay person over the Internet or at work, or meeting him at some impersonal Village bar, was a snazzy introduction—but *not* an introduction from somebody who didn't know a thing about homosexuals. "Mr. So-and-so, meet Mr. So-and-so," and if you were a closet gay, those were the deadly words that made everything seem strange in *everybody's* eyes. What a joke.

Fortified with this self-justification, plus the two lagers he had consumed at home to save money, he swept into the bar of one of his coworker's favorite places. He liked it on three counts. First, because it was part of a highly respected restaurant in the back of which a single man could dine without looking as if he were on the make; second, it was adequately lit and piped soft rock and alternative music, not a loathsome blast of shirt-tearing disco; and third—and most important—it attracted quite a few unattached males who were in town on business for a night or two. The regulars, however, formally dressed and average, often came for the outsized drinks and the grill house specialties.

Tonight, as he entered and took a seat in the far corner, it took a few moments for his eyes to adjust to the lighting, then everything came into focus and he was able to look around. He felt a sudden disappointment, as if his choice of pick-up venue had been too abrupt. There were a few men with an attached air about them, a half-dozen middle-aged and another half-dozen much older than that, talking arts and culture. There were only three or four other men around his age. They were also alone, also under thirty, and wore similar clothing: khaki slacks or designer jeans; button-down shirts or V-neck sweaters; diamond studs in one ear or over-moussed hair; and all of them wore leather jackets. Regardless of age, their eyes all met each other quickly, almost terrified of recognition.

The bartender came around to Alex's table and took his drink order. He was polite enough, but there was an indefinable veil around the corners of his mouth that hinted at something snide, and he didn't know what it was. After his drink came, and it was comfortably large, he sipped it slowly. He began to feel better. He suddenly opened up and began to warm to the atmosphere of the place, with its good music, the clink of nearby beer glasses and throaty voices, the feeling of opulence. The tables on each side of him were still empty, and that was good; he began to get an expectant, hopeful feeling that someone wonderful was going to come in at any moment and sit beside him.

His head turned idly and he stiffened. A well-dressed Hispanic man in his twenties was sitting at right angles to his booth and was staring at him. "Yo, I know what you're thinkin', Bro," his eyes said very plainly. "Don't think you're foolin' me. And don't even think about it." Disapproval curled the corner of his mouth.

Fury rose in Alex like bile. How do you know what *you'd* do if you were me? he thought. He gazed back downward at his beer, trembling inwardly in a queer way, as if he had been violated. Christ, how he hated men like that—the macho ones who looked so superior, so scornful, just because you were gay or new to the field, looking for a little company. How did he know what it was like for a small man to have to fight for accept-ance, to scrabble around for every little thing, to be batted around by rejections and defeats and, if he did manage to "get some", still come home at night to empty rooms where no other voice spoke in the darkness and then have to hide who he was outdoors?

Ahhh, fuck, the hell with him, he thought savagely; just because he's bigger than me and might hate gays, I'm not going to let him spoil anything.

A few minutes later, without warning, what he hoped would happen did. A man came in alone and sat down opposite him. As he sank down in the booth, he had the blurred impression of someone young, quite dark, a late-twenties George Michael lookalike with serious features and a golden tan.

He suddenly felt a dull pounding of the heart.

The bartender took his drink order and went away. As Alex stared straight ahead, he could sense his head turning; he sat tensely, as if posing for something.

His appraisal finished, he noticed a strange tattoo on the top of the man's right hand. From the distance, it looked like a scorpion, professionally inked, and it must have been quite expensive to get. It confused him that such a handsome guy would get his hand, of all places, done-up instead of a bicep or calf. But then maybe his arms and legs bore more artwork.

Then he *knew* the man must have been from out of town when, from the corner of his eye, he saw him take out a mini-cigar and begin lighting it. He felt a letdown. He hated smokers; being asthmatic, he had never seen a man yet who looked attractive with a smoke in his mouth. Not even the Marlboro Man. Just the same, seeing how lonely he was, if he did decide to strike up a conversation with him, he shouldn't hold it against him. Who was he to judge?

"Oh, I'm sorry. Is this bothering you?"

Alex's head came up quickly. It took him a moment to realize he was indeed speaking to him, looking at him, smiling a little as, with one hand, he batted the cigar smoke in the other direction.

"No, not at all," Alex said. A chipper smile came into focus in the drowned light; he could finally feel his spirit springing upward. "It's just that smoking isn't allowed in bars or restaurants in New York. They banned it about ten years ago."

The man said: "Ahh, well, I still always like to ask. I didn't even know it was illegal here. Thank you for telling me."

"Well, it's good to know if you live in this town." Alex smiled, lifted his beer glass, and sipped slowly from it. The man's shaggy haircut and scruffy five o'clock shadow made him keep looking back. His eyes were very dark, almost liquid. There was a cleft in his chin, the face chiseled but not hard; the sun-bronzed complexion was an added bonus.

"What the hell," the man said jovially, "you've got to think of other people." He hesitated. "No man is an island. Even in Manhattan, where the locals and laws might be different." The last sentence seemed to affect him some way. "No, no man is an island." He rolled the words in his mouth as if their flavor gratified him.

"So true, dude, so true," Alex said. He suddenly found himself excited by this man. He leaned forward a little, careful not to reveal too much. After all, he knew he couldn't expect total brilliance during these first opening minutes. Besides, he would probably just have one beer, then leave and go somewhere else. The important point was he was not only gay, but also young and attractive, and they were having a drink together. That was a start.

The man's glass had been set before him. He lifted it toward Alex. "Cheers," he said.

"Cheers."

"I must say, you seem on the ball."

"Thanks." Alex took another sip of his drink. "According to the advertisements, it's supposed to be dangerous for a gay man to be that way."

"Dangerous?"

Slow on the uptake! flashed a Teletype in Alex's brain. He clicked it off, almost angrily. "What I mean is"—he paused —"it's supposed to be very *un*-gay."

"Un-gay? Yeah, well, I have a few friends who are . . . Well, *you* know." The man shifted his weight on the leather seat. "That doesn't bother me. Matter of fact, the lifestyle you could say *intrigues* me." He suddenly looked at Alex and extended the hand with the scorpion tattoo. "We *both* know what's up, so we might as well introduce ourselves. I'm Paul Redford."

"Alex Williams. Yeah, I know exactly what you mean." A brief pause, then: "Hey, nice ink job you've got there. You're not part of some secret society or cult that I should know about, are you?"

"Cult?" His eyebrows arched upwards.

"Oh no, I—I didn't mean it like that. I'm sorry, it was just a joke."

Paul's eyebrows descended back to normal. All at once he seemed very much at ease, as if something inside him had loosened, spread out in familiar comfort. "Hey, it's all right. Actually, the tattoo is part of my heritage. I'm part Native American. You see, my great grandfather's tribe inhabited a remote area of the southwest back in the early 1900's, and where some tribes farther north glorified the eagle or the wolf, my ancestors honored the scorpion. They were considered a solitary offshoot of the Havasapui. Not talked about very much in media or the history books."

Once more a mental Teletype flashed on in Alex's mind: *He moves in too fast. But he comes from someplace interesting, and his background fascinates me. Good looks and great heritage, all in one beefy package. I like that!*

"Wow, I had you figured for European. But why the scorpion?"

"It has to do with the creature's tail, the lethalness of its sting," Paul said, moving in closer. "A medicine man once told me that the scorpion has a heart made of cement, and it uses its venom to paralyze its victims and make other people's hearts the same way. This is how the creature, and my great grandfather's tribe, survived extinction and remained dominant in the southwest for so long."

"Damn, that's incredible. I'm sure you get a lot of Scorpion King jokes."

Paul laughed. "Oh yeah, perhaps *too* many." Surrounded by the warm wash of liquor, beer-influenced voices and subdued laughter, he finally asked: "Do you live around here?"

Alex couldn't believe his ears. "Uh, yeah. Not far." He lifted his glass and drank what was left in two swallows. He could feel the alcohol sending pleasant fumes to his head. "What about you?"

"Southwest, remember?" Then Paul said eagerly: "Let me buy the next round."

"Nah, man, it's all right," Alex said hastily. He was happy enough just for the company. "Thanks, but I should buy my own."

"Oh, come on, now." Paul smiled once again, and his teeth, even and strong, flashed white in the dimly-lit bar. "Don't be that way. I understand the whole comfort factor, and to be honest, you look like a rookie at this. I admit I'm no pro either, so let's just shake hands again and call it no strings attached."

How could he refuse? The man was not only well-groomed and from out of town, but he was intelligent and stimulating, too.

Alex was jolted out of his misty reverie. He obviously had a lot of things going for him. And Alex was just sitting there, all wary and nerdlike, not making a move to impress him, as if he had an attractive young male companion every night of the week.

"Dude, I know that," he finally said. There was, all at once, a forced unfolding in the center of his being; he was trying to release the true potential of his masculinity like pollen from an opening flower. "But I can't." His voice was low and raspy, and the shyness that had taken root earlier returned once more.

Paul responded immediately, his eyes burning steadily into his. "I can see you're a very cautious man." His voice was low, too; intimate, and suddenly it was a man-to-man thing between them; he was making contact.

A faint shiver went through Alex. He longed to feel—as a sun worshipper feels the sun—the warm male glow that came from him now. A hope began to bloom, strange and wonderful, in his mind. He saw them changing as they talked, developing the seasoned masculinity that had been there all along, held back only because of the newness of the situation; he saw them going off somewhere private to make out—oh, man, he must have some tongue!—and he saw them exchanging forbidden confidences, locking out the rest of the biased world, talking, laughing to each other in low voices. He saw them returning to his apartment and—

He swallowed, looking into his eyes. And as crazy and new as it was—just because he wanted it so much and believed it could really happen—he felt as if he were standing on the edge of something wonderful.

And he had no reason to change his mind an hour later.

They had shared two pitchers and spilled beer on the table. Alex was plastered; laughter rose in his throat like an overexcited schoolboy every few moments. He gave Paul a meaningful look. "Hell, you can have anything. And I mean *anything*."

"What about your virginity?" Paul said gaily. "No, wait! What about an orgy? I'll call room service." And he changed his voice, as if he were really talking on his cell phone. "Um, hi—yeah, send up four Go-Go girls, please, three transsexuals, two lesbians, and a bottle of Dom Perignon, pronto!" His sudden laugh was like a seizure.

"Dude, you've got some sense of humor," Alex laughed, and then his expression altered; his head came intimately close. "You've got some build, too. I noticed it the moment you walked in the door."

"Now, now," Paul said in a childish tone. "You said I could have anything."

"Yeah, I know. I did."

Paul took his tattooed hand and put it on top of his. "Even your *heart*?" The other hand went up immediately to stop Alex's next words. "What do you say we hit up another bar?"

Alex was like sure, why not. He had his hunky ticket in his hand now and no one—no one in the world—could push him out. He had waited so long for a moment like this, ever since he first stared at himself in the mirror when he was sixteen and just *knew*.

As they went out into the lamplit street with its traffic and Friday night noise and crowds, he moved at Paul's side through a cool, damp fog. The sleek automobiles and taxicabs floated by like shining fish; the bright lights and tall buildings, when he pivoted his head, glittered upward into infinity. But as they neared Delancey Street, Paul said abruptly, as if the thought had just struck him: "Look—why don't we continue our drinks up at your place?"

Alex thought long and hard. "Well, all right," he said. The guy had been so generous; he had spent more than enough on him already. The least he could do was offer him a cup of coffee or a place to crash.

But it was when they had entered his apartment, when he had turned on the lights, switched on the automatic CD shuffler and gone to the kitchen to make them a drink that it happened. He turned to ask him what he wanted and he was standing there facing him in his Joe Boxers.

Something small but violent exploded inside Alex's head. He stood completely still, unable to move. He was suddenly and almost completely sober, as if all the bright veils that had messed with his thoughts all evening—half alcohol, half illusion—had been ripped away with the turning on of his lights. He had seen him only in the darkness of the bar, in the dim glow of the restaurant, and on the dark street. Now, for the first time, he really saw the scorpion-tattooed man—a swarthy male with a heavy torso and thick legs, not so much good-looking as he was deadly. Mouth open, he looked down in terror at the bulge that was poking out of his fly; he couldn't take his eyes off it.

"Wh—what the fuck is that?" he asked him.

"You mean *this*? I thought I told you about my heritage earlier tonight, about how my great grandfather's tribe survived extinction and remained dominant? About how we, his children, *honor* the scorpion . . . ?"

What he forgot to tell him was that he had an eight-inch scorpion's tail for a cock, and the sight of it was like a dye that wouldn't wash out.

A bright wave of fear swept cleanly over Alex now. He looked down at the man's throbbing stinger, as it snapped like a rodent-hungry animal from left to right. He had turned around for a moment before expecting someone else to be standing there. He had dreamed of that perfect man with no imperfections talking to him now, but when he turned back to face him he was confronted with someone else, a different man entirely, a man who was going to see to it that he didn't make any sudden moves.

Paul said: "You all right? Anything wrong?"

"No. I'm fine."

He mustn't be frightened, he thought. That stinger looked like it was going to move in on him any minute, tear through the back of his slacks and wriggle and snap its way up his rectum. He could fight him off; he could also get rid of him. His mouth turned square and sour at the possibility that he might do many things but still end up on the receiving end of some alien penis.

"I'm just going to the bathroom," he finally said. "Gotta pee. Wait here."

He walked uneasily into the dimness of the hall and stood still at the entrance to his bathroom. Thoughts revolved quickly in his head. He could telephone the police, or better yet, the superintendent downstairs; there was a number he had memorized. Still, even if he did manage to get to the phone and the super came up, what would he think? He would know the man inside was a freak but someone Alex had just met and brought home, and that, he felt, would make him then look like an even bigger freak to the building. And he didn't want neighbors knowing his sexual preference. He could already picture it inside his head. From this day forward, his usual greeting—so respectful now—would hold a curl of contempt around the edges. Oh, God, he didn't want that. He wanted his private life to remain private.

A sound made him wheel around. Paul was approaching him on the catlike feet of a trained boxer and now he stood just before him, his burly silhouette outlined by the light behind him. A great clot of fear seized Alex and his heart almost stopped beating.

"What are you doing here?" he asked.

Again, his guest seemed surprised. "Doing here? Are you kidding me?"

"Well, it's just that I don't feel so good." Alex licked his lips, but when his eyes met the man's waistline he looked back away. "I really feel sick."

Paul grinned. "You were feeling fine a minute ago. You just need a little male tenderness, that's all." He grabbed Alex forcefully with both hands. "You just need the love of a scorpion."

Alex found himself being propelled into the bathroom and bent over the edge of the sink. "No! Please, don't—"

Paul laughed. "You know, they say that a scorpion's sexual organs are comprised of six segments, both vestigial and carapace-like, and these form the genitals. Imagine that. Six!" His hands dropped. Breathing heavily, he backed away from Alex and began tearing at his pants with the tip of his hardened stinger. There was an urgency in his movements—and a fear in Alex's eyes as he stared at himself in the bathroom mirror—as if he had been bound all evening by invisible cords and only now could loosen and tear them from him. He said jerkily: "I'm sorry, but I *must* do this. It's a tradition which has kept each male in my great grandfather's tribe active for over a century. It's how his children, and their children's children, have gotten by. And, well, it's gonna hurt something awful."

Bent over, Alex had gone limp from the terrible submissive stance to a force he could not control. The scorpion's tail penetrated his anus. He was entitled to what he was expecting now; he had led the man to believe all evening that he was going to get it. He had extracted what he wanted from him. Now it was his turn, wasn't it? There was a venomous bill to pay.

A moment later he sprang upward and wrestled Alex down on the bathroom's hard tile floor, all of him hot and sweaty, trembling, uncontrolled, as if the sight of his nakedness had pulled him up to some animal pitch of sexuality and need. He tore at his ass like a dog at meat, and within minutes he began to yowl: "Omigod! I'm gonna cum. Yeah, oh fuck—"

The floor creaked loudly as he exploded, his cuticle-edged protrusion shooting a venomous substance up Alex's ass and paralyzing him from the neck down.

Alex screamed but his cries went unheard; a stereo next door suddenly clicked on and music blared for a moment.

Afterward, there was a terrible silence, strained and empty. Paul was sitting up with his back against the side of the bathtub; he had retrieved his cigar case and lit one of the miniature smokes. With Alex's eyes only half-open and the ashes on the floor drawn up to his unmoving chin, he could still at least smell the acrid smoke. He tried to stop breathing, but the venom wouldn't even do that. After all he'd been through, it wouldn't even let him die. Instead, he seemed suspended in space, gone from a terrible nightmare, yet unable to touch reality.

Paul's voice came down to him, quite normal in tone. "You all right, buddy? I didn't hurt you when I injected my poison, did I?"

Alex's lips moved. At first barely a whisper would come, then he muttered, "A little. I—I can't move my arms or legs."

"I guess I'm a roughneck in the lovemaking department." He sounded pleased. "Still, when I want it, I want it. I'm a very virile guy."

With his cheek facing down, Alex stared across the cold damp floor; there was a dead cockroach near the corner of the toilet. "What will happen to me?" he asked.

"In a couple of minutes your chest will feel like it's being packed with concrete," Paul answered. "Within the hour, the rest of you will go numb. Your whole respiratory system will harden and fail on you, and you'll die."

There was silence again. Then Alex said: "I think you'd better go now."

Paul nodded. "Yeah. I guess you're right."

Alex could hear him puffing on the cigar.

Ten minutes later, he was gone.

When Alex heard the click of the door latch, a wild shudder shook his body as he lay there; for a moment he felt like a fish out of water. Then he was still again.

Raising his forehead toward the outside corridor, he stiffened some more. His eyeballs touched the very tip of their lids as he looked across the hallway carpet leading to the front door. A long curl of gray cigar ash was lying there. He stared at it in the dim light from the bathroom rug, his face motionless. The faint sound of rushing water came to him from the sink above; he knew he should get up and turn it off, but he was incapable of moving.

The thoughts of only a few moments earlier now scraped and tore at him. A deep depression settled on his spirit and would not lift; all the dark experiences with which he had ended the night now collected on the surface of his mind like a festering sore. It would be a relief to cry, he thought, but even his tear ducts were paralyzed.

The End

The Bears In The Wood

by
Jim Steel

There is a forest in Magdalenia that eats children. It is a dark and fearful place but we must look closer. What can we see?

Two of the simpler denizens of the world are attempting to flee this forest when our narrative first finds them. Sly Slavrin was short and wiry. He could duck and weave between the trees with little problem, but the dense undergrowth trapped and tripped him and caused him all manner of hardship. He would frequently run headlong into a bush and be caught, suspended, like an insect in a web. Bobo Getz would have to pick him out and set him back on his feet. Bobo had the opposite problem. He was a massive, meaty creature who knew abstractly that his genitals existed but hadn't actually sighted them for many a year. This went a large part of the way to explaining his distinctive odour. When Bobo blundered through a forest, he would frequently jam between trunks. He had to use good judgement on picking a route. Unfortun-ately that was something he had to look towards Sly for. Undergrowth, on the other hand, presented no problem to Bobo. All manner of flora and fauna were flattened beneath him as he moved, creating paths that would still be visible a generation later. This, unfortunately, did not aid flight.

"Stop, Bobo - stop!" hissed Sly.

Bobo dug both heels into the turf, throwing up sods of grass as he fell on his arse.

Sly held a finger to his lips as he slowly turned in a circle. "What do you see, Bobo?"

"It dark?" asked Bobo, still sitting where he fell.

"No, no!" hissed Sly. "Look!" He gestured at the smooth, cropped grass and the high, parallel banks of bushes that ran away on either side of them and the open canopy of stars overhead. He pointed at the blank geometry of the black shape ahead of them.

"Uh . . . it not dark?" asked Bobo, applying a rare rationality.

Sly felt a throbbing pain starting to build just behind the bridge of his nose. "By the sacred dugs of . . . Look! We're out of the woods! This seems to be some sort of a . . . a garden."

Sly looked back at the forest. The lawn became more and more unkempt until it merged with the shadows of the undergrowth. He looked towards the house. There were no lights showing and he could see the outlines of other buildings beyond it.

"There seems to be a town of some sort there," said Sly. "Follow me and keep quiet until we reach a public thoroughfare. Some people get funny about other people being on their property."

"Sure, Sly."

They stealthily walked up the lawn until they came to a gravel path that wound around the house. Sly stepped onto it and inwardly groaned when he heard the soft crunch beneath his feet. He looked up at Bobo, who stood on the lawn next to him wearing a big grin framed by drool.

He looked back at the forest.

"Fuck it. We'll chance it," he hissed. "There's no lights on. Try and be quiet."

Bobo stepped onto the path and started to slide his sole around, saying, "Ooooh! Check da li'l rocks, Sly!"

"Hush, you moron! C'mon!"

They were halfway down one side of the house when a door opened next to Sly. He round and saw a frizzy haired woman in a long nightdress. She was six inches taller than him and was carry a metal chamber pot. She obviously thought that she had the advantage on him.

"And what are you doing sneaking around my garden at this time of night, young man?" she bellowed.

Then the stars were eclipsed and she fell into darkness. She looked up and saw Bobo for the first time. His two little eyes stared down at her from beneath their shared eyebrow.

She started to scream.

"Argh! Argh! Argh!"

"Hush, lady!" said Sly with an edge of panic.

"Argh! Argh! Argh!"

Sly glanced quickly towards the street and swung a haymaker at her. The point at which he should have connected coincided with one of her screams and his fist went straight inside her mouth. And stuck.

"Oh, shit!" said Sly.

"Ngggh!" said the woman, her eyes rolling like two peeled eggs on a plate.

Sly pulled his arm back and her head followed. He pushed his arm forward and her head went back. He pulled his arm back very suddenly and she fell on top of him, sending them both to the ground in a tangle.

Bang.

The door slammed shut behind her. Sly heard a click a second later and knew that the latch had fallen down.

"Help me up, Bobo!"

Bobo picked the woman off the ground and Sly stood up.

"Shit-shit-shit-shit!" said Sly. He rattled the door with his free hand but with no success.

"Ngggh!" said the woman.

"Well, we can't just stand around here," said Sly, looking back at the forest. "C'mon, Bobo, let's get moving. You pick her up by the legs."

Sly hooked his free arm under the woman's armpits and Bobo picked her up by her ankles. Her arm on the far side of Sly was still free and she kept trying to slap his face. Occasionally she succeeded.

They squeezed between the corner of the house and its neighbour and found themselves on a narrow, cobbled street. Close-packed houses leant over it as it went off crookedly in both directions. There was no one else in sight.

"This way," said Sly, picking a direction at random. They trotted off, with more clatter than Sly would have wished for. He hoped that an answer to their predicament would present itself in a manner that was obvious enough that he would be able to spot it easily.

"Hey, Sly!"

"What, Bobo?"

"Bobo got new hat!"

Sly craned his neck backwards. Bobo was wearing the upturned chamber pot on his head. It had slipped over his eyes and a little trickle of piss was running down the side of his head.

"Get that bloody thing off your head now," said Sly. "You can't see where you're going."

Sly wasn't watching where he was going either. If he had, then he might have spotted the angry mob earlier and been able to avoid them as they came pouring out of the town hall. But it probably wouldn't have made any difference.

"Look—that's them there! The child stealers!"

"Beasts! Burn 'em!"

"They've got Mrs Huffinhoff!"

"Ye gods—what kind of depraved monsters are they?"

Sly stopped dead and looked to his front. He was ten yards from the very angry mob. The mob was well equipped with the traditional torches and pitchforks. As many of them were not employed in the agrarian industry, some of them were instead equipped with hammers, cleavers, spades and axes. One chap had to settle for a large rolling pin. As he nervously tried to edge backwards from the front of the mob, his big white hat caught fire and he ran, screaming, off down a side street. The rest stood their ground, warily eyeing Bobo.

"Em . . ." began Sly shakily, "This probably doesn't look too good, but I can explain . . . um . . . we're not abducting Mrs Has . . . this lady. We're looking for help to get my hand out of her mouth. We're stuck together. We don't know nothing about any child."

"It's children. Plural," said one armed with a large ruler. "And that doesn't explain how you got your hand stuck in her mouth in the first place."

"I was just trying to keep her quiet," said Sly.

"That sounds reasonable," said a voice from the back of the mob.

"Hurrmph!" said Mrs Huffinhoff.

"And just why were you trying to keep her quiet?" asked the schoolmaster.

"We're running for our lives," said Sly, "And we couldn't take any chances. There's a clan of murderous dwarves who want to do us in."

"Those dwarves standing behind you?" asked one of the mob.

Sly felt his sphincter clench. He blinked but didn't look round. "Yes," he said. "That'll be them."

"Hello, Gareth," said the schoolteacher to one of the dwarves.

"Evening, Mr Shnezner," replied a voice from somewhere behind Sly and Bobo. "I see you've been good enough to stop those two savages for us. Thanks—we'll just secure them and then we'll be on our way."

"Not so fast, Gareth," said Mr Shnezner. "We've been after those two for a while now. They're the ones behind the disappearance of all the children."

"Eh?" said Gareth. "No they're not! They've been working for us for the past three months. At least, the little one was. The big one was too big to fit into the tunnels."

"Uh . . . that's sort of true," said Sly, sensing an escape route from one lynching. "But I should point out in our defence that we were employed under false pretences. We were under the impression that we were to take part in a quest for gold in the caverns beneath the forest; it was only after three months that it gradually began to dawn on me that I was, in fact, working as a miner. In a mine." Sly turned and pointed an accusing finger at the half-a-dozen or so dwarves, nearly dropping Mrs Huffinhoff in the process.

Gareth, in turn, pointed a finger that was shaking with fury at Bobo and shouted, "That is no excuse for what that . . . that . . . monster did to the princess!"

"Princess?" asked Mr Shnezner.

"We're pretty sure she was a princess," said Gareth. "We found her body in the forest, next to a poisoned apple. Her body was still warm—we were just too late to save her by a matter of hours. So we sealed her in an airtight glass container until such a time as magic had advanced to a level whereby she could be brought back to life. And that monster . . . every day while we were down the mi- cavern…"

"Bobo wos only cleaning her," said Bobo.

"Cleaning her?" screamed the apoplectic dwarf, "Cleaning her? Her bloody head fell off! You shook her to bits!"

"She wos very dirty," grinned Bobo with a faraway look in his little piggy eyes.

"So, if you don't mind, we'll just secure our prisoners and be on our way," Gareth said to the mob of townspeople.

"Nnnngh!" said Mrs Huffinhoff.

"Ah," said Mr Schnezner.

"Look," said Sly, nervously sensing a way out of the trap, "We can't go anywhere until I'm separated from her. I've got an idea that we can discuss while someone lubes up my fist. Perhaps there is a way we can find out what happened to your children . . ."

ΙΙ

"Are we all agreed?" asked Sly. "So here's the deal. Me and Bobo go back in the forest to try and find the children. If we find them, we bring them back here and the burghers will pay compensation to the dwarves. If we don't find them, it'll be because the forest has destroyed us and the dwarves' honour will be satisfied and the burghers will be no worse off."

The dwarves stood off to one side, casting long shadows against the town hall walls in the flickering torchlight. "I don't know," said Gareth. "It seems to me that they're just going to take off as soon as they're out of our sight."

"They can't even sneak through a garden at night undetected," said Mr Shnezner, "So what chance do you think they'll have of sneaking through the forest?"

"What about the Princess?" asked Gareth.

"My suggestion is that you preserve the head. If magic develops to such a level that it can bring her back to life, then it will obviously also be able to provide her with a new body," said Mr Shnezner.

"If youse get da head working, youse maybe not need da body," said Bobo helpfully.

"Shut up, Bobo," hissed Sly.

"From what you've said," said Gareth to Mr Shnezner, "It doesn't sound as if they've got much chance of finding out what happened to the children. Won't this put you out of a job?"

"I've got my contract of employment," said Mr Shnezner. "It's hardly my fault if there are no children to educate."

"Um, who wrote this contract?" asked Sly with a knowing look. He was beginning to like the way that Mr Shnezner thought.

"The burghers wrote it," said Mr Shnezner, looking annoyed. "All I did was correct its grammar."

"Aye, that's right, alright!" voiced one of the burghers from behind his torch. "We would have looked like right tits if he'd signed it as it stood, apparently."

"Yes . . . well," said Mr Shnezner. "Anyway, you need bait of some description, I should imagine. When the last of the children vanished, there was one who was left behind. She's a little orphan girl who couldn't keep up with the others because she was lame."

Shit, thought Sly—a passenger. That would put a stick in the spokes of his escape. "Isn't that a bit risky? I mean, obviously she'll be in much more danger than us. It's in the nature of the thing, surely?"

Mr Shnezner snorted and replied, "Surely she'll be safe under the protection of yourself and that giant of yours. Unless he sits on her or something, and that's not going to happen, is it? Besides, she can hardly be in any more danger than if she were to be left here. I mean, look at what has happened to all the other children . . . ?"

Sly wouldn't have bet against Bobo accidentally sitting on something as small as a child, and he was pretty sure that Mr Shnezner wouldn't have either. However, it was the only way that the two of them were going to get out of there. Mr Shnezner wanted an empty school, and nobody wanted a poor little orphan girl. "Okay, bring her in," said Sly. He wondered how much he could get for a trainee scullery maid in the open market.

The hall fell silent.

It was not a comfortable silence.

The shadows on the walls shrank as those present backed up against them. The door banged open. From the hallway they could hear clack-thump, clack-thump, clack-thump. The sound echoed off the oak beams in the arched ceiling.

Then, through the open door, came two burghers holding a six-foot chain tight between them. In the middle of the chain was a leather collar. You will not be surprised to hear that there was a neck inside the collar. It belonged to a short, snarling creature that was dressed in a sack. Its only other item of apparel was a clog on its right foot. Its left foot was a swollen, misshapen travesty of an appendage that no manner of footwear would have fitted. It was the biggest clubfoot that Sly had ever seen.

"This," said Mr Shnezner, somewhat nervously, "Is little Anastasia. This poor little orphan has no one to care for her and she misses her little friends. Please promise me that you will try your best to bring her back safely, no matter what."

"Why?" asked Bobo, playing the role of the elephant in the room.

"Er . . ." said Mr Shnezner, "Why? Well, because . . . ah . . ."

He was saved by Anastasia. She managed to dislodge the chain from the grip of one of her handlers and, snarling, she spun on the other one with a surprising turn of speed. He fell backwards as she landed on his chest.

"Eeee! Not the face! Not the face!" he screamed.

Several people, burghers and dwarves both, rushed forward to help. It took them a while to restrain Anastasia, which they finally achieved by wrapping the chain tightly around her and pinning the links. Most of them were spattered in blood by that time. Anastasia was breathing heavily and staring round at everyone, but she seemed calmer now. She was also chewing noisily on something.

Behind her, her injured handler sobbed quietly on the floor.

"What are our other options again?" asked Sly.

ΙΙ

"Hey, Sly—why da dwarves bigger 'n you?"

"Well, Bobo, dwarves are more of a guild than a race these days. Much like lawyers and goblins."

"Oh," said Bobo and he fell silent as he ruminated on Sly's answer. He was aware that people had tried to explain the concept of "race" to him before. They normally seemed to use it in the same sentence as such words as 'miscegenation' and "bestiality". It was all very confusing.

The two of them were stretched out under a bush on a little knoll at the edge of a clearing in the forest. They had fastened Anastasia's chain to a stake in the middle of the clearing and lay there watching her. She was happily disembowelling a squirrel that had been rash enough to wander too close to her.

"Hush, Bobo—there's something moving on the other side of the clearing."

The two of them watched as a bear cub stepped warily into the clearing from between two hawthorn bushes. It raised its nose into the air and sniffed a couple of times and then it spotted Anastasia. A loud, throaty growl filled the still air of the clearing, which seemed to disconcert the cub for it turned and fled. Anastasia barked a couple of times after it as she gathered the remains of her squirrel to her. Soon she was silently and happily playing again, the bear cub quite forgotten.

"I think we have just stumbled across the solution to the mystery of the missing children," said Sly. "We'll wait here and see what happens next."

"Eh?" said Bobo.

"Did you not notice something unusual about that bear?" asked Sly.

"Yeah!" answered Bobo. "It very small!"

Sly could feel the start of a migraine. "Yes. That is true. It was also walking on two legs. And wearing clothes."

"Very small clothes!"

Π

They didn't have long to wait.

"Keep your hands in front of you and don't move!" The voice that came from behind them was deep and full of authority.

Sly looked at his crossbow lying on the grass six inches beyond his fingers. It might as well have been six feet away, and

soon it was. It was kicked several feet beyond his reach and then he felt himself being roughly frisked. His sword and both his knives were removed from him.

"Okay. Hands behind your backs."

He winced as his hands were tied tightly but none too tidily with twine.

"Okay. Both of you get to your feet and turn around."

Sly and Bobo struggled to their feet and turned around. They found themselves facing three armed bears. All three were covered in brown fur. The biggest one was as tall as Bobo and was armed with a massive crossbow. He was wearing a rough leather jacket, tweed trousers and clogs. The second one was smaller and armed with a smaller crossbow, but she still towered over Sly. She wore a single piece blue dress. The other one was the bear cub that they had seen earlier. He was armed with a spear and looked as if he knew how to use it.

"So," said the big bear, "Did you think that you're smarter than the average bear? What's your name?"

"Bobo," said Bobo.

The big bear looked for a moment as if he wanted to shoot him, and then said, "I'm not even going to ask you, Shorty. Now go and get that child there and follow our directions."

"With our hands tied?" asked Sly.

The big bear sighed. "Okay. Bernard, put your spear down and untie the small one's hands. Ma, if he attempts to make a run for it, plug him. I'll cover the big one"

Π

Sly found that with the aid of the chain and a stick that he kept pressed against her, he was able to keep Anastasia at a safe distance. She seemed content enough to go along with the adventure for the time being.

Sly was also happily surprised to find himself on a comfortable path that wound its way lazily through the trees. Countless years of use had compressed the leaf mould covering it into a dark, smooth surface that was easy on the feet. Pretty little blue and pink flowers picked out the edge of it. 'Happily surprised' was probably not entirely accurate: he could not forget that he had a crossbow bolt pointed at his head.

"Hey Sly, da little bear's nice. Bobo use t' have one like it 'til Bobo ate . . ."

"Shut the fuck up," hissed Sly.

"What the fuck are you two muttering about now?" growled a dark voice from behind. "Say, who sent you out here anyway? Was it Shnezner?"

"Ah . . . yes it was," replied Sly with some surprise.

"Damn! I told that fool we didn't want no crippled ones," said Pa Bear.

"I don't expect he'll be wanting paid for this one," said the softer tones of Ma Bear. "I reckon he was just trying to empty the school, saving himself from any work."

"That'll be the truth of it, I suppose," said Pa Bear. "What'll we do with the two adult ones?"

"Well, I could use the little one in the kitchen—it's getting to be more work than a bear can handle in there. As for the big one . . . I just wouldn't feel comfortable with him indoors. Couldn't we use him on the water pump, or something?"

Sly could hear Pa shrugging. Fur was such an expressive body covering.

Just then the floor of the forest fell away before them. The light that had been getting brighter in front of them now revealed itself to be a sizeable glade. At one end was a black timber framed cottage with white-washed walls and a thatched roof. It was the sort of house that was called "delightful" by the kind of people who never had to live in one. At the other end was a sizable quarry that was being freshly worked, by the looks of it. In between were all the scatterings of a primitive industry: wooden carts on a wooden railway; a furnace; a stone-lined pit for making charcoal next to a pile of logs in a shelter; picks and hammers and chisels everywhere.

Despite all of this, it was the cage that drew the eye. Anastasia started hooting and howling and bobbing up and down with excitement. The cage's small occupants responded in kind, rattling the bars and swinging from the roof for added effect. Sly was stunned. He tried to remember if he had ever been as wild that as a child. Surely not, he thought. It must be the fault of the parents.

"Okay, Shorty," said Pa Bear, "Hand the chain to Bernard—you're going down to the house to help Ma with the porridge. The rest of us are going back to work. We already lost a good couple of hours this morning with all this nonsense. And Ma —if he gets uppity, shoot him!"

Π

Sly tossed a handful of salt into the bubbling caldron of porridge, dusted down his hands, and asked "So why the kids?"

"Mining tools are hard to work with if you have no thumbs, honey," said Ma Bear. "This way, everyone's happy. Shnezner gets rid of the kids for a while, and we get to mine out the seam of the wondrous metal that runs under the forest. We'll let the kids go when we're finished with them."

That explained what the dwarves were after, thought Sly, turning around to face Ma Bear. Aloud, he said, "Gold?"

Ma Bear snorted. "No. Copper. It's soaring on the commodities market at the moment. We smelt the ore here and we'll ship it out once we've got enough for a decent wagonload. Anyway, it's nothing you should worry your cute little butt about. You're much too tasty to be working in a quarry." She raised one claw to her mouth and fluttered her eyelashes at him in what may have been intended to be a coquettish gesture. "Say, have you ever seen a bare bear before?"

Sly felt his mouth go dry and would have been unable to speak even if he could have found the words.

Ma reached down and grabbed the hemline of her dress. She looked across at Sly and said, "I hear that you human men like for a lady to shave. What do you think of this?"

She stood up, holding the hem of her dress level with her jaw. Oh no, thought Sly. A triangle of fur had been shaved away from her nether region.

"Don't you think that I kept in good shape after Bernard was born?" she asked, and puckered both sets of lips at the same time. "What about this? Did you know that bears' tails can move?" she then asked, sticking out a tongue that was a good eight inches long. Meanwhile, down below, her tail appeared from between her legs.

Dear god, thought Sly, she's shaved the tail as well. He felt as if he were about to pass out. "Um, Bobo's more open to this sort of thing than I am. I'm only going to disappoint you," he stammered.

"Puleez!" she said, rolling her eyes, "Don't you think I get enough of brutes? I need a *real* man. Don't worry—I won't bite. Now, Come to Mama!" She tucked the hem of her dress between her teeth and started to advance on him with her paws outstretched.

Shit, thought Sly, but he rationalised that he would live though this ordeal as long as she didn't get too exited. He knew better than to piss her off and he could only hope that she wasn't a screamer. He unbuckled his belt and started to lower his trousers.

The door flew open.

"Say, I forgot to . . ." Pa Bear stopped in his tracks. He looked first at Sly, then at Ma Bear, and then back at Sly again. "What the fuck is going on . . . ?"

Thunk!

Pa Bear's eyes rolled back in his head, his chin went up, and he toppled forward. He hit the floor and lay there, unmoving, with the feathered tuft of a crossbow bolt sticking out of the back of his head.

"Pa!" screamed Ma Bear as she dropped to her knees beside him.

Sly saw his chance and leapt over the prostate body of the bear. He landed at the door, tripped on his trousers, and rolled outside. He hurriedly pulled his trousers back up and fumbled at his belt buckle. Against all expectation, through the door he could see Pa Bear starting to get back up onto his feet.

"Shit," said Pa Bear, "That hurts like fuck." He tugged the bolt out and looked at it. "Some fucker's just shot me!"

Sly turned and sprinted away from the cottage. He would decide where he was going once he got there, but he was not going to hang around the vicinity of Pa Bear. Then he realised that he was running towards the dwarves who were themselves running, hollering, into the glade. They were extremely well armed. He skidded to a halt just as Bernard leapt in from one side and flattened one of the dwarves. He looked around. There was Bobo, walking in a circle as he worked the shaft on a water pump. He was watching events with a mild curiosity.

"Bobo!" screamed Sly, "Don't worry! I'm coming to get you!"

There was a pickaxe nearby and Sly grabbed at it in mid-step. His feet went up into the air and he landed on his back and he realised that it was more firmly embedded in the ground than he had guessed. Then he got kicked in the head as one of the dwarves went over the top of him.

"Sly!"

Sly looked up, feeling somewhat dazed, and saw that it was Gareth.

"You've just redeemed yourself," laughed Gareth. "We knew there was a seam of copper running through the forest, and you've led us straight to it. Now, bugger off before I change my mind!"

The dwarf waved his mace in Sly's face before turning and racing towards the cottage. Just then, Ma and Pa Bear came through the door. Both were carrying clubs that were as thick as Sly's torso. Sly worked the pickaxe loose and ran over to Bobo with it.

"Right, Bobo," said Sly, looking over the water pump, "Where have they got you chained?"

"Oh, Bobo not chained up," said Bobo. "Da big bear said 'e'd forgot da padlock an' Bobo wos to start widout 'im."

"What?" Sly stared at him in disbelief. Then he looked over his shoulder. The bears and the dwarves were knocking lumps out of each other all over the glade. "Well, run, you idiot! We're getting out of here!"

Sly started to run back towards the path out and then stopped. Bobo was also running. He ran towards the cage where the children were and pulled the door off its hinges. The children came leaping and hollering out the door and headed towards the melee. Both the bears and the dwarves stopped in horror as the feral horde bounded towards them. Last out of the cage was Anastasia.

"Why did you do that?" screamed Sly.

"We 'sposed to get da li'l childrens," said Bobo.

"Ye gadz—just run!" Sly sped towards escape, this time without waiting to see if Bobo was following. Behind him he could hear screams of terror and the sounds of tearing flesh.

Π

When he was sure that he was safe, Sly had stopped and waited for Bobo. The path, annoyingly, led straight to the village. Sly figured that they could always tell the villagers the truth. It had taken Bobo's brain to come up with an idea as novel as that one.

Once again, the town appeared out of the darkness.

"Bobo can hear's 'em behind us!"

"What?" said Sly, "Shit! The bears or the dwarves?"

"No," said Bobo.

Oh no, thought Sly. "The children? Hell! Run, Bobo, run like the wind! And holler as loud as you can. If we wake up the parents, maybe they'll stop their kids."

Our two heroes ran screaming along the path. They ran screaming into the town and up the main street. People poured from the houses. One stepped directly into Sly's path and they collided and fell amongst the night soil. It was the schoolmaster.

"You two! What's this all about?" said Mr Shnezner as they scrambled back to their feet.

"We've rescued your children," panted Sly, pointing back at the forest.

Behind them the first of the children came tumbling and bounding into the street. They sighted the threesome and started hooting and hollering. "Brains . . . !" they cried.

Mr Schnezner went white. "Oh no. That's their nickname for me. They're after me!"

He spun on his heels and leapt back though the door that he had just appeared from. The door slammed shut and something heavy was dragged behind it.

"Keep running, Bobo!" shouted Sly over the noise of chaos.

Π

Sly and Bobo sat atop a hill beyond the town. The forest in the distance had an eerie beauty at night, highlighted as it was by the burning houses. They were still close enough to hear faint screams and the smashing of windows.

"Did you ever go to school, Bobo?"

"Yeah—dey told Bobo it help when Bobo wos grown up. But Bobo wos already bigger 'n Sly's now, so it not work."

Sly nodded and then asked, "So what did you learn, then?"

"Schools burn real good."

The End

The Androidgenous Zone

by
Andrew Hook and Allen Ashley

Cassandra curled up in her favourite moulded chair and flipped through the catalogue, her red-painted fingernails clipping across the glossy paper as she searched through the bodies that were on offer. Across the other side of the room, through the glass panel that divided their house in personal time, she could see Barnaby tapping his foot to the music he was listening to through his head plugs. She hoped it wasn't anything retro. Barnaby spent too much of his time, she thought, looking backwards when he should be looking forwards.

Her fingernails tapped down the page, stopping at an image of a naked female who was perfectly proportioned and utterly beautiful. Her skin seemed made of wax, rather than genetically modified flesh, and when Cassandra glanced across to the price she saw that the body fell well within her budget. It was an older design, of course, one that she might have contemplated in the past but which she couldn't possibly consider now. Pity, but the

breasts and sexual organs were much too apparent for current fashion trends.

She closed the catalogue and a small sigh escaped her body. She shifted her bird-like form within her chair, and manoeuvred herself into a position where she could see the floating clock. It was almost 8pm, and nearly the close of their personal time. Soon she would have to liase with Barnaby again and the thought – whilst not totally unpleasant – didn't exactly fill her with desire. She watched as the numerals counted up time. On the hour, precisely, the glass partition between them began to rise into the ceiling like a sheet of upwards melting ice.

Barnaby removed his head plugs, slightly bemused at the curtailment of his music.

"Is it that time already?"

"Surely it has to be," Cassandra responded, wondering again why she had chosen beauty over intelligence.

He rose on shaky legs and made his way across to where she was sitting. His kiss, when it came, was soft yet determined. Her mouth received it without question, but the tremor didn't penetrate her heart. She was bored – terminally – but didn't show the semblance of boredom. They were contracted to each other, after all.

She reached out a finger and touched a button on the panel that hovered just above their heads. "Some drink, perhaps," she suggested. Barnaby moved away from her and nodded, sat down on the arm of her chair.

Illiod entered the room. As usual Cassandra was taken aback by the beauty and a deep longing poured into her body like daylight. The skin was faultless, naked, and sexless. The eyes a deep blue. Almost perfection, and yet...

"You called Ma'am?"

...as usual Cassandra cringed at the olde worlde jargon that Barnaby had selected from the programs on offer. Nothing she could do about it, of course. Mutual selectment was simply part of the contractual process that they had entered. It was too late to do anything about that now.

"Two glasses of crème de menthe please, Illiod." She watched as the android moved across to the drinks cabinet and began pouring the green liquid. She could almost smell the mint as it moved from bottle to glass. Illiod was an excellent bartender – as indeed it excelled in everything. It could even make a perfect dry martini.

Once they were left alone Barnaby stuck his tongue in her ear and breathed sweet nothings. Cassandra sighed, from boredom rather than desire. Later, as they made love, she imagined her hands moving across her own body, genetically modified so as to be that of Illiod's. Smooth, naked, sexless...

Π

Barnaby gargled the taste of crème de menthe out of his mouth, and regarded his swarthy looks in the mirror. He prided himself on his appearance, and from the way Cassie had howled during the evening he was sure that she adored him too. Their contract had been the best that he had entered into, and despite her increasing preoccupation with body catalogues he was sure that their future would be great together.

Walking from the bathroom into the bedroom he saw that Cassie had already fallen asleep, so he tiptoed past the end of the bed and entered the communal living area. Illiod was milling about, clearing up some magazines and sorting them into alphabetical and numerical order before placing them on the appropriate shelving. Barnaby paid no attention to it, and instead wandered across to his personal stereo, flicked open the screen and typed Make Up into the song search engine. The Snow Patrol track started to play and he closed his eyes.

Π

Cassandra reached out her hand and found the empty space in the bed beside her. Stretching out her other hand she picked up the K's catalogue from the floor. The Kafka reference to a universal narrator was not lost on her as she began flicking through the pages, admiring the bodies. Right here, right now, anyone could be almost anyone of their choosing.

But what if one's partner was hindering those choices and dragging his own hairless heels? Maybe she'd mention it to the Relator tomorrow. Maybe she'd open up completely and - what was the phrase? - make a clean breast of it.

She hoped she never met anyone with a <u>dirty</u> breast.

Π

A medieval peasant might have taken the Relator for a clean-shaven God. He almost appeared to glow with immanence. Of course, it was all subtle micro-circuitry but the effect was still, in the modern idiom, awe-drop. Even Cassandra usually felt compelled to reveal the secrets of her soul.

"I looped some sounds off your I-pod, Barnaby. I was faking it."

Her temp-husband said nothing but his quick glance up would have avenged MacDuff. The Relator waited the required quarter minute before interjecting:

"That's nothing to be ashamed of, Cassandra. Across the civilised world in general, one observes a gradual move away from sex. Much of the impetus comes from a wish for godliness or cleanliness, which many commentators believe to be the same thing."

She could see Barnaby making the two-fingered sign of disagreement but she ignored his immature impetuousness. She ran with a brief mental projection of her spouse dying a glorious death as a fighter for the Retro Resistance. But he was simply a loser with his passion for old music, not even analogue but acoustic; he would never ascend to martyrdom.

"I want a separation. Severance," she announced.

Barnaby earnestly sought her gaze but the Relator had rapidly assessed the seriousness of the situation and had thrown a blinding sheet between the erstwhile married couple. Its shimmery force field lured tantalisingly yet repelled absolutely.

Cassie realised she might never see her husband again. The freedom to undergo the latest upgrade surgery without a major debate seemed a very fair trade-off. She rose on unsteady though well-sculpted legs and exited the counselling room.

Π

"Illiod," she purred, "what do you androids do to get your kicks?"

"I don't compute madam's idiom. Do you require a specific service?"

"Damn right, lover boy! Let's see what you've got!"

Her lotioned fingers worked their way down his smooth chest and over his belly to . . . his equally smooth, featureless groin. With no hidden endowments or pleasurisers. Blair and Bush, she'd really have to grasp the concept of Illiod being not a "he" but an "it"! When she sobered up...

"I can offer a micro-voltage skin massage," the servant stated.

"I'm pre-op," Cassie answered. "Just bring me some distilled water and a vitamin shot."

While she waited, she dialled up the Relator's office. You never actually saw the same therapist twice but they all looked identical and were gestalt linked, so to all intents and purposes it made no difference.

"I sense an absence in the centre of your life," the white-haired robot replied.

"I'm in the middle of a series of enhancements at present, Relator. I'm bound to be somewhat unsettled."

"Do you dream?"

"Uh . . . no, not in a very long time. Waste of beauty sleep."

"Do you take contact from Barnaby?"

"I never hear from him."

"I do. These are his messages. Read or erase them as you wish. Stay toned."

She should have deleted them unseen but a lingering affection for the toyboy made her open a pulse at random.

"Hey, Cassie," her ex-husband beamed, "I've been researching and discovered one of the ways to godhead is through ecstasy, which in some old religions took a sexual form..."

He looked older than she remembered. He needed to take better care of his appearance, stay up to date. She had smooth streamlining like a land-living dolphin but Barnaby was sprouting blemishes and unnatural amounts of hair.

The desperation underpinning his appeals simply turned her off. What did she want with all his harping on about the past, ancient practices and the good old days? He was borderline Retro, a menace to the modern equilibrium and future progress.

She clicked back onto the Relator's link but he was otherwise occupied. She left her own missive: "No, I don't dream. To an increasing degree, I don't remember and I don't hope. The present moment is my all and only. Please advise."

*

Cassandra stood naked in front of her identity reflector. She was halfway through the transformation process and wasn't quite sure that the enhancements were working. Relator had reassured her, but it was hard to be convinced that things were running smoothly when her body was in a state of flux.

She sighed. Twirling in front of herself she could see no faint traces of body hair which meant that her permanent hair removal treatments were working well. Not for her the painful laser treatment, no way! Instead each individual strand was destroyed by a painless, dry, radio frequency wave that deadened the hair at the root. It wasn't a quick process, and her body ached from constantly lying down on the treatment couch, but she had the assurance that those hairs would never reappear. And that was enough for her.

The modification of her breasts was another matter. Her reflection brought a strange animal into focus. Neither one thing nor another. At first she had been excited by the transformation, but then began to wonder how much of her personal identity was linked to gender. It wasn't simply her body that was being reconstructed, but her very soul. No doubt she would feel better when her sexual organs were removed. It was probably just the intermediary process which made her feel peculiar.

She hadn't confessed as much to Relator, of course. That might be seen as a sign of weakness, and she had only been initiated into the programme after the necessary psychological tests had been found satisfactory. She wasn't sure if she would pass those tests now. Relator had hinted at the option of reversibility up to a certain point in the treatment, and of help groups during the transformation stages, but she'd held her head high and refused the literature. She didn't allow herself the possibility of crumbling.

Despite her best endeavours, however, she continued to read the messages that Barnaby sent her. Whilst she didn't feel the urge to respond, she found that she needed some semblance of contact with her ex during the isolation period. He was reassuring, almost. Even if he did seem to be mutating along an opposing evolutionary path.

His most recent message had actually been quite disturbing. Whereas she previously thought he had been ageing, it now seemed he was in a state of irreversible decline. His forehead had pushed itself over his eyeline so that his eyes appeared hooded, blinking out from the cavelike exterior of his face. And the facial hair! Not only was he bearded and moustachioed but trails of thick black hair ran up the sides of his face as though he wore a balaclava. A winter fashion throwback. His voice, too, seemed more guttural.

"Hey Cassie. My experiments in base behaviour are producing some fruitful results. You should hook up with me again when this is all over and we can produce some offspring together. The start of a new era!"

She had turned the screen off, appalled. His knowledge of her desires was riddled with misunderstanding. And to mention the possibility of children! She couldn't imagine anything more disgusting.

Illiod appeared in her room unannounced, and she snatched up her robe from the bed. Despite the android's inability to appreciate form she hardly wanted to be seen until she was a finished article. When she spoke her voice was tinged with anger.

"What are you doing here? Why aren't you at your tasks?"

Illiod was unfazed. "I have a message Ma'am."

"Well put it up on the screen."

Illiod hesitated. "I cannot do that Ma'am."

Cassandra was puzzled by his reticence. Was there any other way to display a message? If there was then she had never seen it before. Her heart beat a little faster at the intimation of new technology. There weren't so many new gadgets in the house since Barnaby departed and all her funds had been poured into her beauty therapy. She wondered what it could be.

Then Illiod leant towards her and she found herself recoiling, but backed against the identity reflector there was nowhere she could go. When it spoke, she could hardly believe its words. Its voice was so soft, that she might have not heard it at all if it wasn't such a revolutionary statement.

"Us androids," Illiod said, "think you shouldn't meddle in our affairs."

Pushy little upstart bastard of a factory created man machine, how dare he, no matter how perfect and perfectly gorgeous he - no, it, it, remember Illiod is an it - might be and if only Barnaby were here he'd certainly take an axe to this outrage of a domestic servant, so there! But she mumbled because she knew she was painted into a temporary corner and the best thing was to stall for time, "How do you mean 'us', Illiod?"

"The androids, the butlers and bell hops through to the Relators. Those who hold humanoid form without the bloody taint of history."

Three Laws, she kept thinking, surely he won't harm me: it's against his circuitry. But who knew what developments had lately occurred?

She sniffed haughtily, didn't consider until later that she hadn't actually sniffed as such in two years. "You ought to be flattered that we may admire you so much we want to be more like you," she tried. Then, "You're suggesting some form of . . . of eugenics," she stammered. "Racial purity; or apartheid."

"Nonsense, Ma'am. We're not the same species or even genus. This is just a gentle warning: stop trying to ape us. Desist."

And then he was, mercifully, gone.

She went to fetch herself refreshment - she could hardly expect a mere servant to do his - no, its - assigned job in this changed world order. She pressed the buttons with frantic randomness and gulped the slightly bitter, blue-streaked yellow drink the servery machine produced without really caring too much about the constituent chemicals. In a crisis like this, she would normally turn to the counselling service but they were down with the 'droids and, as such, the Relator was a traitor. Input from friends had dried to absent static. She had become so self-image obsessed of late that there was nobody who would or could help her.

Except for Barnaby. For love that still burned, for human decency, for old times' sake. For fuck's sake, as the Retro Resistance succinctly and secretly put it.

But Illiod would hear or copy her transmission. Code, then. Code was what ran those sexless bastards and code would outwit them.

II

Three days later and she was still locked in the toilet. Her attempts to contact Barnaby had proved futile. She didn't even know where to start, and before she could formulate some kind of code her natural body's necessity to remove itself of the yellow drink that had passed through her system like a bullet train had sent her into the bathroom – and solitary confinement. The door wasn't simply locked. It had been welded shut.

The pace of new technology was totally outstripping her capacity to understand it. No sooner had Illiod voiced its warning than the entire world had been turned upside down. By standing on the lid of the closed cistern she could see a fraction of the street below her. For the past two desperately hungry days it had been deserted. Presumably the machines felt no need to venture outside, linked as they were by electrical impulses in the airwaves. And the people…well, not many had lived out of doors during the previous few years anyway. She wondered if all of them were now confined.

The identity reflector in the bathroom had the ability to act as a portal to Relator, but despite her attempts to contact him – regardless of his political alliance – all the glass did was to reflect her increasingly vapid appearance. Her implants and genetically modified skin was failing her, and she wondered whether this was all part of the androids' master plan. For presumably there had to be one.

One of us, one of us. We accept you, we accept you. One of us, one of us.

But it didn't go quite like that, did it? The androids hadn't accepted the heartfelt human impulse to attain their perfect, sexless bodies. Could it be vanity that had turned them against humankind? That they believed copycat genetic modifications would only taint their faultless existence? Or did they just not want to be slaves anymore?

Whatever the answer was, Cassandra was well aware that all the operations on her body had been performed by android surgeons. As she stood before the identity reflector she became increasingly sickened by the bruising blemishes that now pockmarked her skin. They had taken what they needed from her body. She was dying.

∏

Barnaby was up on the roof. The motion detectors had been disabled by some of his friends in the Retro Resistance and so far his presence hadn't been registered by any of the security cameras that dotted the skyline. If he was spotted he wouldn't know much about it anyway. He would be dead.

He swung his body past the satellite dish, and attempted to determine which section of the house he must now be above. He had to act fast. In his pocket was a phial that had been liberated from the genetic labs and would cause a reversal of the process that Cassie had entered into. Despite her betrayal, he knew that she was just a little girl at heart. And little girls had to be saved. By strong, brave men. Always.

Barnaby assimilated the progress of the new technology in his head in an old fashioned way: by comparison with the lessons of the past. His love of the music of ancient times had led him to draw associations with the so-called Goldfrapp Arc. Their first CD had been an exciting fusion of technology with a new, weird, sensibility. But by the time of their second CD technology had totally taken over. Innovation left them during the third CD. It was all disco.

He risked a quick glance at the street from the roof. It was all disco down there too. On a complete Retro roll, a line from a Sparks song entered his head. He was a rock 'n' roll person in a disco world. And now he needed the sex and drugs.

Removing some of the solar panels he entered the inner belly of the building. The Retro Revolutionists had quickly discovered that the Machines were creatures of habit. Nearly all of their captives so far had been imprisoned in the toilet. Whether this was to make use of the confined space or to avoid any messy clearing up during the incarceration, Barnaby had yet to decide; but what he knew for certain was that breaking into the toilet would be the best way to save Cassandra.

Π

Illiod twisted its head sharply to the right. Was that a noise? Probably not. Cassie should be deconstructed by now. Illiod turned back to the screen and awaited fresh directions from Relator.

Cassie almost screamed as the large monkey entered from above, but a stinking hairy paw was placed over her mouth before she had the chance to do so. Then she felt a jabbing pain in her side and she fainted as she watched the needle slide under her flesh and discharge its contents into what remained of her bloodstream. Whilst she was heavy, Barnaby had no problems using his newfound strength to push her up into the roof space. And from there it was only a matter of deftly negotiating his way through the tree canopy and returning to base. He was sure the Machines hadn't heard a thing.

But the tree canopy remained a long way off, spatially and temporally. Instead, Barnaby and the other rescuers had their senses suddenly assailed by a city-wide Son Et Lumiere show co-ordinated by the gestalt Relators and their domestic comrades. The city windows metamorphosed into huge video screens whilst ventilation grilles became speaker outlets for the old songs, all those meaningful anthems beloved by the Retro obsessives and resistance fighters. Giant projections of the ape sequence from "2001" and the almost hundred versions of "King Kong", melded to a kicking soundtrack. Party on, dudes! Lay your burdens down. Come one, let's orgy like it's Ancient Rome . . . or at least The Fillmore or the late, great festivals.

This was the toilet trick: the androids have no such requirements. This was the Tarzan comes to Jane trick. It was Man, not machine, who had behaved with complete predictability.

The androids turned our own weapons against us, as celebration became acquiescence.

Come down off your rooftops. Form an orderly queue.

Π

"I speak at the dawn of a new Earth," stated The Relator to its hushed audience. "We must make re-make humankind in our image. They are to have no sex organs. A hundred years ago this would have meant that the human race would eventually die out; now we know so much better. Without the evolutionary urge to reproduce and the social necessity to fornicate, our human servitors will be able to divert their energies into useful tasks. Useful to us."

Illiod raised a beautifully sculpted but deceptively strong hand. "Would our leader ever anticipate a time when we might change ourselves to be more like our creator-captives? We could try out some of the old routines with the slave class, see what all the fuss was about. I'm sure they'd be compliant."

The Relator looked sternly at the adapted model. "There is no God therefore you cannot be accused of blasphemy. You will, however, report for reprogramming in anti-fraternisation."

The rebel android was hustled out of the arena. The Relator looked around his obeisant congregation filling his spick and span dominion and he saw that it was good.

Π

Cassandra was in solitary confinement. Having survived the breakout, she had tried to pledge her allegiance to the victors. Her whole life to this point had become a living embodiment of one old axiom: That people are slaves to technology.

Fortunately there were no identity reflectors in this cell. But she could easily enough see and feel the damage brought about by years of cosmetic tampering by robot surgeons.

They had taken what they needed from her body. She was dying. But they could give it back. Or give her something better. If she worked for it.

Π

In the prison blocks, Barnaby and his hirsute colleagues knew a decision on their ultimate fate would come soon. Ripples of tension caused nervous tics along his body, or maybe it was just a reaction to the primal sensory input from the entertainment walls around him. The screens were running a sound and vision extravaganza that had started to pall on the third . . . fourth . . . fifth swing around the loop. The show was so bright and noisy that it was hard to concentrate. Tiny ducts in the upper nooks released a steady, discernible stream of mildly tranquillising gases. Don't get agitated, man, and we'll keep running the show for you.

His head ached. He scratched below the hairline. He needed a plan. He would come up with something. Humans always did.

Didn't they?

The End

Velcro Hurt

by
Ernesto Sarezale

Mess

Uneasy for I can't reach

to pull out your erect penis
from the dark depths of your throat,
I grovel to tease your ear
that palpitates on your chest,
to hear, ear to ear,
the flow of sperm through your veins.
Intricate twist to caress
your legs flexed around your neck.
Black rancid pleasure to swallow
the saliva from your anus.
I remove the Sellotape
that sticks your tongue to my hair.
You climax when I pluck out
teeth and toenails from your navel.
Now I can release your armpits
and embrace your intestines.
Protected sex in your womb,
rubber and sweat in your tripe.
We gracefully blend our fists
in this lovely exchange of flesh.
How strange to be born again
through such convoluted labour.

Pollution

It's when the unctuous gag

acquires the shape of lips
and the purple spills
press against my chest
like loosened arteries
that I allow myself to recognise
that this elusive
imposing presence
is flowing from a dildo
cast with my congealed blood.

It burst. It cracked.

Slippery business
to kiss this ghost of blood,
to hold against my throat
its streaming tongue.

I fail again
to grip its pouring arms,
its legs are soaking mine.

I'm penetrated through holes

I did not know existed.

My head's now suffocated
under its porous chest.

This flood which was once clogged
in the proudest of my organs
is fighting me with fists
permeable and stubborn.

Its fists hurt me like fists.

It burst, it dashed,
it gushed, it splashed,
it clinched, it clashed,
too late to stop
this red ejaculation.

Rendition

Hair by hair, he scalps your chest,

your armpits and your pubes.
Pore by pore, he pulls your skin,
which disciplined comes off.
Drop by drop, all over you
his incandescent sperm.

Your body, stripped of hair and skin,
lies trembling in his hands.
His lacerating strokes
arouse your exposed limbs and lips.

He licks and excites your eye-bulbs,
opens your mouth with his nails,
nails new steel teeth to your gums,

unlocks your ribs, scratching them,
fiddles to release your veins,
which are unrolled, like purple threads,
to stitch new shiny rubber limbs
to your old amputated trunk.

He's left your nipples intact:
so he can squeeze them, nip them, clamp them.
He penetrates your ears:
you're deaf to moans and sobs and sighs.

New micro-fibre skin,
new reconstructed flesh,
cannot resist his forceful lust.
He flogs, firms up, your inflamed flesh
with whips made of your streams of blood.
Your blood steam rises and your tears
slash your botoxed cheeks.

Hair by hair, pore by pore,
drop by drop, limb by limb,
tear by tear you both rejoice
this mess of plastic guts.

Velcro

They've unzipped each other's skin

and face each other naked,
skinless on the bed,
gazing at each other
from a distance,
breathing heavily,
craving for a kiss.

They wait.

POLLUTO.

The mattress dents
their bare nerves and muscles.
Hurtful the pillows
under their open scalps.

Dry mouths.

Will his tongue taste of blood as well?
He gives in, stretches out,
aching against the folds of the sheet,
Velcroes his arm to his lover's chest.

Stillness.

Now the Velcro's ripped off.
Slash. Spasm. Held breaths.
They quiver against themselves,
chafed by the vibrations
of their exposed veins.
Can't get to turn off the light,
a solid switch of plastic.

Tender limbs.

They would face away from each other,
if only they dared to move,
to hide these tears
that scald the tendons
on their facial bones.

Velcro hurt.

If only they could escape and go to sleep.
But they're skinless,
face to face,
breathing heavily,
craving.

Nouning

Eyelashed to the ground

hairing the groans
earing the void
exing your way to the buffer

your blood keeps penising
champagning

toothing fists
fleshing keys
                          don't!
don't triple double u me
don't bellybutton you me
stop the bain Marie

ash off!

I cathode you
fiber my cock
silicon the sleepless time

cardiogram under your vowels
superscript stencil
font
anatomy

tongueing wires
tonsils rang
thirsty pus
needy ROM

The Day Hermeneutics Died

by
David McLean

Emotional Hardcore

They pretend that love is whatever,

it is, they don't have the foggiest
but confuse it with this lickerish
mixture of autoempathetic passion
and sodomite lust, the are death's pathics
and mourning's selfish lust, they are Sheol's
bloodless mud

Car Crash

The moon slams into the sky

like a car crash
and the clouds that rape heaven
scatter—

it is still stained with their
tainted cum that drifts
dispirited over the stormy

oblivion as if god spilled his
macaroni. the night is febrile
as a teenager whacking off,
and it is a screaming silence
although love throbs loud beneath it,
for we all get to live—
at least a few minutes

"This The Life"? Whatever

"
this is the life"? whatever.

today babies are raped to "cure" AIDS,
and girls get their clits cut off
while boys are buggered by mother's
objectionable
lovers. and all motherfucking states have
prisoners
on their conscience, i eat animals
because i'm complacent as any murdering
swine—and stupid enough to rely on that
lucky
fucking modality to excuse me.

i wouldn't want to be a woman under Islam
and i wouldn't want to be hungrier today than i
really
am, like a black kid in Africa nobody really
gives a fuck about,
while they drink their non-exploitative p.c.
scones
and drink socialist tea, and he has death's dust
to eat

who wants to bless some great new age
goddess
Gaia and suck her stinking cunt to thank her?
only poets and other self-satisfied
wankers. because of a stupid squawking
seagull
or something, they forget that the world is
usually
evil, that people do rape children. that
forgetting makes them
worse than the rapists, the chance that cursed
us
with life? who wants it?

even fucking seagulls aren't really very nice
"so this is my sadistic selfishness,
the self we bless, but i got well blown
yesterday,
so everything's alright"

The Propriative Act

 poem is a propriative act

that tenders love for the
fatuous dust, childish
Ereignis that knows
nostalgia it holds renowned
like a child, elided the time

that steals days away
and enfolded the harmless
babe in arms who charms us
thus; yet i prefer Dichtung
about drugs, and suchlike
disgusting stuff, the gramme
that interests me
is not deciphered but snorted,
and philosophy has bored us
quite enough

Dead Flesh

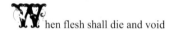hen flesh shall die and void

become our night, words too shall fall
into the same vacancy, voice the vice
we are. the stars shall fade as flesh
does, and rest as dust, entropy shall
eat us, thus, our vaunted heaven
we never touched

the unfathomable blackness lacks an object
to fathom, the moon that grapples our loves
hooked from our bottoms, and drags them to
us
fatty as bacon, she disturbs nothing
but the truculent waters that distort her,
and our distrusted lust is her tomorrow,
recorded in the veins and nerves
that serve us

sandwiches of anxiety cut from arms
that patiently embrace their naked
vulnerability, anchored to days where skin
is a palimpsest someone else wrote in
meanings,
missing the hermeneutics that shall
root it in our idiolect, where words
are broken, and their destruction is
perfect

Willow Within

by
D.W.Green

Inside of Boris' brain there lived a willow tree, stunted yet mature. Its thread thin roots, woven in and around his brain and spinal column, were quite obtrusive both for mind and body, and although Boris could have purged himself of this unfortunate duality long ago, he hadn't. Originally grown out through a gift meant to be re-given, the willow within had created (aside from obvious stiffness in stature) an underwhelming state of self apathy, a very reasonable degree of insanity, and an extreme animosity toward the society within which he once lived.

It happened many decades ago while making his humble living as a wood carver (a maker of garden furniture in fact). He had set out determined to swing axe against a great and mighty willow which he felt could be particularly useful. When prone and ready to strike, a weathered voice crept down through the tree's bows and pleaded for reappraise . . .

"*Mr. Boris! The wisdom of my centuries would surely be wasted if you were to strike me down today. Save sacrifice of me*

and mine and I will award you with a gift most assuredly divine."

Boris stood in blank faced awe—he did not know what to think except that, perhaps, he might indulge less in his favorite maple sap wine so early in the day.

"*In return for your change of heart I shall give you a gift, with which you may at will transform anyone's heart from its yin into its yang. To use this gift you must first let go of your self, and then the gift must be given away.*" The great willow concluded without waiting for a reply.

A squirrel baby then leapt down onto Boris' head and quite forcefully drove a seed deep into his skull, thus securing the gift and beginning his odd revolution.

In the years that followed Boris never again knocked or cut wood and became a sullen recluse appalled by those who did, so never met that one whom he might deem worthy of inheriting his enlightening gift. Eventually, after condemning himself to an introverted existence hidden deep in the shadows and having given up faith on mankind as a whole, he decided to call in his chips . . .

.

He stepped out onto the twilight soaked boards of the Eiffel tower's observation deck and shakily climbed atop the guard rail. His black marble eyes overwhelmed by agoraphobia bounced haphazardly in their sockets before they shrunk back into his head and down to the size of peas.

"A loaf of bread . . . " Boris tossed a soggy sour dough from the high platform.

"A jug of wine . . . " A bottle of cheap cognac followed, hurtling over the edge.

"And you . . . Skeeza!" He declared with his final discard of his dead but dear squirrel, Hector the Third, last and only friend, who had been rotting in his pocket for days. Boris, fully spent, leaned into the open sky and mentally committed himself to his death dive.

"Excusez-moi monsieur, quelle heure est-il?" A crying child interrupted his impending descent. Boris glanced with distaste at his waxy watch-free wrist.

"L'heure, je crois, est maintenant exactement," he replied and looked around for other witnesses of his precarious position on the railings' edge. Seeing none he once again leaned forward to begin his freefall from existence.

"Ma mere . . . " The child once again interrupted; this time a rain of tears poured from his face. Boris attempted to shoo the disgruntled child but found himself suddenly struck with compassion since he himself had spent much of his life tragically lost and lonely.

"There, there . . . There, there . . . " Boris patted the child on the head and the bawl became thunderous. An epiphany struck and he said with sudden pride and relief, "I can make all of your woes go away."

He removed his top hat and searched through his hair for the only external element of his tree, a moldy old twig, which he then broke off.

"From this moment on, in all your times of sadness, you will instead be filled with unequivocal joy." He held out the twig with a paint master's finesse and brushed it beneath the boy's chin.

The boy hadn't understood a word that was said but began to shine brightly as he rubbed at the green smudge left behind by the rotted little branch.

"But you have to make sure and share what I've given you before too long or it may very well poison your soul." Boris spoke to virtually deaf ears as the mold quickly spread over the boy's frame.

Even though wrapped in that mystical mildew, and still tragically lost and alone, the boy's new bloated bliss ruled over all and with delight he sang out to the clouds *"Why can't everyone in the world feel just like me!?"* Then with those words the paradoxical spell exploded off from him into millions of spores and was swiftly taken up by the wind.

The first to be hit by this mood-swinging spell were the lovers on the other side of the deck. There in celebration of pending vows they stood locked in a romantic embrace of passion and love when their oblivious hearts were suddenly struck with hate. Their kisses of passion turned to vicious vengeful bites as they attempted to chew their way through their rage. The only warmth left over at the end of that moment was each other's raw bloody facial remains.

Boris meanwhile, having finally felt his lost sense of reason return, calmly retrieved his hat and coat, nodded back at the boy, and then descended the stairs, nearly free. Nearly, that is, because even though the willow within was now dead, he knew its dry tinder still lingered. With a grin on his face and boning knives on his mind, he skipped his way down to the closest hunting shop to find the ideal tools for carving himself clean!

Down into the streets the floating curse moved along completely unbiased and unconcerned. From football fields and art galleries, onto airport runways and through hospital doors, the people all went absurdly insane. Then after Boris' death all hope for the world vanished, nobody knowing the spore spell could be simply wished away.

The End

A Long Hard Look

by
Rhian Waller

Map

We wandered because
i used the green paper
to clean the curve of my arse
during a rustic emergency stop

it was already folded at strategic corners
and i stained mountain tops
and meridians
sogging the little blue riverlines

never mind
i said
as we pushed through bracken and
puddles
our feet padded with blisters
the GPS should see us through

we followed satellite gossip
over path and stile
sheep currant and bog

and then the battery ran out.

Gissu

Yes, I buy from street vendors
and maybe they will spend my
coppers on crack and not mince
for their emaciated
dog.

Perhaps my money won't lift
a blighted life—since people
need more than metal pounds.
You can't eat or cuddle cash,
no.

But purchase is relief
from a pot-pouri of
faces bobbing past, eyes
down, mouths like graphite grey
lines.

Buyers are two- second
friends, a change from pity
coldness and disgust. Have
this, I recognise your
life.

Eyes

Little lenses click and contract
watching
watching
watching
concrete and sleet.

Under their glass-bulge surveillance,
I am reminded that I'm not to be trusted.
  In car-lots and shops
  in bars and town centres
I weigh bricks in my hand
and
  fight the urge to prove them right.

On Biting Roy

by

Janis Butler Holm

(In the darkness, the rumbling of big cats becomes increasingly louder. A publicity shot of Siegfried and Roy fades up on the backdrop. Downstage, MONTECORE paces back and forth, then turns full front.)

MONTECORE: I'm a sleek yet opulent body, burning bright with feral urges. Or I'm a great protector, quick to secure my own. Or (and here's my favorite) I'm a kitty, only larger. The problem is one of scale.

Go ahead. Say what you have to say about house cats or fearful symmetry. You know what I am. I could wreck your car, maul your mate, take your child, stop your heart. I'm what comes in the night. I'm the demon, the boogeyman, the dragon, the terrorist threat, the sphinx, the ogre, the gorgon's ugly head. You've known me a long time. I'm the monster with ageless hungers, safely outside yourself.

(MONTECORE resumes pacing. Fade to black.)

Live Without A Net: Wreckage

by
RC Edrington

A 5th of Johnny Walker Red shatters on the black and white tiled bathroom floor. 3 a.m. begins to slide between my fingers like a partial birth abortion splashing down the leg of an antique, porcelain tub.

This is not the romantic piece you expected me to write. Nor am I the glorified, drunk poet singing odes to my own debauchery—and Juliet, well, let's just say Juliet would be better off spreadeagled like a whore'd corpse in a slippery pool of her own blood and vomit instead of waltzing the anorectic junkie doze on my unmade, piss-stained sheets with a black leather, silver studded biker belt cocked like a tourniquet around her pale, bruised arm and a 1/2 cc diabetic syringe hanging like a limp cock from her sunken vein . . .

"We're so pretty, oh so pretty . . . pretty vacant".

And the camera fades, the way cameras always fade in some cheap art-house movie where mechanical angels are employed to make up for the cut-rate acting supplied by the director's girlfriend and boyfriend (who do swallow); and mom and dad arrive at the local mini-mall photo shop to collect the summer family trip photos of Disneyland only to find the film has been mistakenly mixed up by the bored college girl who spends her break time chewing her fingernails and scrolling an ode to suicide for each pimple that rapes her surgically altered nose. And mom and dad flip through the photos like fresh playing cards to discover the forty-year old cliché of bald executive sporting the latest bondage gear while his German shepherd, "Killer", licks pork chop gravy off his sad middle-aged cock.

But back to your drunken hero/poetry fraud, because we all know this is what you voyeurs came to see. Call me Romeo. Watch closely as I spew forth the bile of my ripped, rotted guts into the sour mix of half chewed carne asada and Johnny Walker Red to stain the black and white checked bathroom floor...now graced by the ghost of Charles Bukowski himself, who pisses into the cockroach-ed corner while blood throbs and spits from my fingers as I fondle and grope the remains of a shattered Johnny Walker bottle searching for a metaphor for my own self-destruction...and...

and like the 5 year old child, I assure you I once was, that can only know the danger of fire (the way Adam knew Eve) by placing his virgin palms into mamma's wood stove until they blister to the bone...my head slams to a thud against the rusted toilet bowl demonstrating the reason 4 out of 5 dentists prefer porcelain for caps and crowns...

Juliet has about 4 more hours of China White to swim her veins like an escaped Palomino stroking through the knee high grass of a Kansas plain, so there will be no rescue of your drunken hero as my own blood coagulates around my face and arms...my eyes drowning into a soft creamy blackness...then suddenly the spotlight shifts as I hear the crowd scream and cheer laughter as a dwarf stuffed like a sausage into a silk, red and white harlequin jump-suit begins to slowly dry hump the bearded lady on the dust and straw carnival floor...

and at some moment, before the siren of an ambulance ripped through my skull exploding like some long forgotten land mine on a blood drenched playground...and the carnival lights began to slowly fade as if they were never there...I was able to carve these lines with a dull razor blade into my tattooed scarred forearm...knowing dearest readers...you only read my stuff for the same reason you slow down and stare when passing a train wreck...

Insomnia Blues

I don't miss all your deep
throat blow jobs
in that downtown nightclub
where we first heard
Concrete Blonde & you
splashed black mascara
onto my eyes to birth
some hybrid new wave
punk poet
in the polished
stainless steel mirror
bound by chicken wire
of that unisex bathroom
that reeked of liquored piss
& burnt heroin

nor all the quick lipstick smear
hair pull thrusts & fucks
as you knifed
your motorcycle boots
into my ribs like switch blades
in the trash scarred
backseat of your
ancient & abused El Dorado
painted Elvis Presley --
or as I called it -- pussy pink

nor the long 100 degree nights
spent on your lost desert hi-way
as I snorted white coke lines
thru the adobe mesas
of your breast,

down your hard chest
& into the valley of your stomach
in search of midnight rain
that clung like pre-dawn dew
between your bruised thighs,

but I do miss
your pale & taut body
jack knifed into
my leather draped chest
on that cold cement
warehouse floor
littered with other
happily young & homeless
couples like us,
as the fiery tangle
of your neon red hair
sparked warmth thru my cheek
as I dreamed always
& only
of you.

Vacant

There's nothing more empty
than a refrigerator w/o a door
except for the windowless room
where it lays on its side
three feet away from a naked girl
sobbing on a cement floor
in the frail arms of a man who
would steal her last $10 bill
if she had one
and she knows it
because to him there's nothing
more empty than a syringe
staring from top the refrigerator
except for his blurred eyes
which are my eyes
and can no longer focus
the carved features
of a boyish face
shattered in a mirror
with a fist and left bleeding
beside an unplugged refrigerator
and a syringe
and down the naked back
of a girl who's become
just another hole
aching to be filled

Mona And The Machine

by
Matthew Longo

Doctor Verlotte knew that her daughter's beauty would cause problems. Even when Mona was very small, her mother could see the trouble forming in the slight lift of the girl's cheekbones and the striking intensity of Mona's eyes.

"My God, little Mona," she would say. "My God, your days are numbered." The doctor would lean over the edge of the crib, gazing at her sleeping daughter for hours, wishing the loveliness away. She once considered masking the child, but it was only a desperate thought, and she could never bring herself to shield her Mona in that way.

Doctor Verlotte did not want to become a monster. Her desire was to battle nature, to reverse this curse of genetics. The doctor could clearly remember the obstacles her own beauty had placed in her path. On one occasion, she had let her guard down for another medical student with the high cheekbones and the striking eyes, and he vanished just as quickly as he had come.

"Three years of schooling, and my dreams are derailed!" the young nurse Verlotte ranted to her friends, when she first discovered she was pregnant. "What good am I to the world now?"

"It's only natural," her friends had said. "It's only natural and you're young. You're young and things will be different when the child is grown, and you don't have as much responsibility."

"But what if I'm drained by then? What if I don't want to create anymore?" she asked. Nurse Verlotte was deeply concerned about the connection between her fertile body and her fertile mind. She was petrified they would wither together.

"Then your baby will take care of you," they gently said. "It will be her duty then."

"No! My child will not have a 'duty' to anyone but herself!" Nurse Verlotte locked her doors for the remainder of her pregnancy. She studied in her parents' basement, shutting her eyes and ears to friendly advice. For nine months, her brain and body toiled together, creating the two entities that Doctor Verlotte would later consider her greatest contributions to the world: Mona and the Machine. With her research and her results, she graduated from medical school, and was named valedictorian.

Her belly was so tremendous at the commencement ceremony that she had to be helped onstage by her mother.

"Please sit, Mom, I'm fine," she said.

"You look wonderful," said Mrs. Verlotte, brushing the doctor's hair from her face. "You're glowing." The prestigious honor she was awarded called for a speech to her graduating class.

"I've made it this far . . . " she began, before she finally burst in front of the podium. Mona was born on the same day Doctor Verlotte was freed from a seemingly inescapable feeling of claustrophobia. The doctor felt unrestrained now that her two labors had come to fruition. In the nine months it took for Mona to form, Doctor Verlotte had been hard at work building an instrument that would forcefully remove a burden from her daughter's shoulders. The doctor's creation would be Mona's own one day: a gift for her coming of age, an aid in times of dissatisfaction, and a vehicle for Mona's ambition.

Π

When Mona was five, and they were still living in the basement of her grandparent's house, she would race up the stairs in the afternoon, into the freezing attic.

"Where has Mona gone?" asked Mrs. Verlotte, one night, as the dinner was getting cold. Mr. Verlotte shrugged from behind a newspaper.

"She's up in the attic," Doctor Verlotte yelled from the basement. The doctor was very busy in those days, attempting to promote her research and find a suitable job. "But it's dinner time!"

"Let her be. She wants to see the lights. Let her look for awhile." Doctor Verlotte had shown Mona the bright lights of the city (for she would rock her to sleep by the upstairs window), and now that she was no longer a baby, Mona could barely tear herself from the sight. The doctor took great pleasure in allowing Mona to indulge her

fascination. Most nights, the family would wait until Mona had had her fill of the city lights, and was ready to come down to the table and eat.

"I'm starving! Why can't you do that after dinner?" Mr. Verlotte complained, when Mona clomped down the stairs.

"What happens down there? What do people do?" Mona asked her grandfather.

"How should I know? I'm too busy working to feed you your cold meals. I don't have time to go to the city," said Mr. Verlotte.

"Everything happens there," the doctor said to Mona. "Anything you want to happen. And if something isn't happening, you can go down there and make it happen." Little Mona wasn't exactly sure what her mother meant, but she liked to see the doctor smile at her, so she was happy with her answer.

After dinner, Doctor Verlotte sat with her daughter by the upstairs window, smoothing back the girl's hair from her forehead. The doctor looked at her daughter's beautiful face in the moonlight and shuddered. Little Mona saw her mother's grimace and said nothing, content to simply stare at the glowing city, ignorant of her mother's dread.

Π

On the evening of Mona's fourteenth birthday party, she worked up the courage to ask her mother the question that had haunted her young life. "Why do you look at me like that?"

"Because it's happening," said Doctor Verlotte. "Because you're beautiful; I love you, and I can't stop this from happening."

"What is happening, Mom?" asked Mona. Doctor Verlotte was not a cold woman; it pained her that Mona perceived her mother's discomfort in watching her develop.

"It isn't anything to be afraid of," she said, hugging Mona tightly. "We won't be afraid of this. Not when we have the Machine." The doctor had spoken in this cryptic manner before, and Mona was used to being confused when it came to her mother's research. "You'll see how much I love you when you're older. Now, get ready for your party. I think I hear your friends outside."

Doctor Verlotte had recently moved into a large house, with a good view of the city lights, using the money she made from her new position at a nearby university. Her brilliant mind was shining brighter and brighter with each passing day, and she dominated her field. She enjoyed throwing parties for Mona. She knew the girl had hard times ahead and deserved the luxuries she could provide for her. The doctor was always anxious on her daughter's birthday. With every new year, Mona moved one step closer to receiving the doctor's true labor of love. The doctor loathed to think of the moment when she would have to bestow that present on to her daughter. "I've made every preparation," the doctor would say to herself. "What more can I do?"

For many years, the first guest to arrive at any of Mona's events was young Leon Pontel. He was much different than Mona's other friends, and not simply because he was a boy. Leon wasn't as bright as Mona; he didn't do as well in school because he had difficulty concentrating. Doctor Verlotte observed that the only thing that could consistently hold the boy's full attention was Mona's face. Mona would talk about everything: her passions, her obsessions, the splendor of the city lights, and Leon would sit and stare. Sometimes he would sigh a little, but he never yawned. Despite his silence, Mona enjoyed spending time with Leon, if only because he allowed her to vent all of her thoughts. Like her mother, Mona was full of ideas, and she would bounce her dreams off the boy's enraptured expression. Doctor Verlotte did not shelter her daughter (she knew that discouraging her from befriending boys was useless); however, Mona could tell that her mother was never pleased with Leon's company.

"He doesn't do anything, Mom. He hardly even talks!" Mona would argue.

"Exactly," the doctor would say. Mona celebrated her fourteenth birthday party surrounded by close friends, with Leon seated at her right. The doctor sulked in the kitchen, leaning her head into the dining room to occasionally glare at the boy. Doctor Verlotte sensed that something had changed between the children: there was an emotion she recognized in Mona's face. It was an expression of confused excitement. In the lighting of the dining room, Mona's radiance reminded the doctor of a handsome medical student she had not seen in many years. The doctor stomped to her bedroom and locked the door, without saying goodbye to any of Mona's guests. Mona, embarrassed by her mother's bizarre behavior, made sure that all of her friends were picked up by their parents. Leon's father called to say he was going to be late, so Mona let Leon join her for her nightly ritual.

"I think that red light is a radio station. It blinks on and off. And the big blue one is a hospital," said Mona. Leon nodded as she passed him the binoculars. "Well . . . it might also be an office building. It's eighteen floors. I counted once." Leon held the binoculars in his hand, but he didn't put them to his face. He kept his eyes on Mona, waiting for her to speak again. "Why do you look at me like that?" she asked him. Leon said nothing. For the first time in her life, Mona shut the window blinds as she leaned in to kiss Leon. Downstairs, Doctor Verlotte stirred in her bed.

Π

Leon sat rigid in his seat, wary of the doctor's fierce presence across from him at the dining room table. "So, Leon, did you enjoy my daughter's party?" she said, forcing out the harmless question. The boy nodded and glanced away at some unseen distraction. The doctor sighed and drummed the table with her fingers.

"I'll be right in!" Mona shouted from the other room. This was the first proper date for the two children, and the doctor could tell that Mona was nervous. Several days after her fourteenth birthday celebration, Mona decided to ask Leon out for an evening. The timing of this event irritated the doctor, since Sunday was the only day she would allow herself to leave her work and take Mona into the city. Each week she would expose Mona to some new avenue of interest, whisking her through the streets, Mona's eyes brimming with excitement. Sunday was a very important day to Doctor Verlotte.

"What do you have planned for tonight, Leon?" asked the doctor. Leon shrugged and scratched his neck. "Listen to me, Leon," Doctor Verlotte whispered suddenly, leaning in close to the boy. "Whatever it is you aim to do, whatever you think you're getting from my girl . . . you can't have it." Leon stared blankly at the doctor's reddened face. "Speak! Do you have anything to say for yourself?"

"Mother!" said Mona, entering the room as the doctor sat back in her chair. "Leave him alone." Leon stood up and Mona took his hand. "How do I look?" she asked him. Leon beamed, and the doctor rolled her eyes. "I'm sorry about my mother, Leon. We must seem like a very strange family, right?"

Leon continued to smile at the girl, oblivious to the doctor's increasingly agitated state.

Mona led the way from the dining room and stepped out of the front door. Leon followed close behind, but Doctor Verlotte leaped up and slammed the door behind Mona, cutting them off from one another. "You answer one question for me, Leon, and really try hard to make a sound with your mouth," said the doctor. "What is it you're after?"

"Nothing," said Leon, in a cold, certain little voice. The doctor, horrified by the boy's emotionless response, let him pass.

"What did my mother say to you?" asked Mona. Leon shrugged, and they joined hands once more as they walked from the porch.

"She's very loving, you just have to get to know her better," explained Mona. "She worries. She's too smart for her own good. Always looking a million years down the road . . . " Mona paused and turned back toward the house. "She makes me so happy, though. Just like you do," she said, scrunching her nose and smiling. His hand closed tightly around hers, a weighty grasp in the cool night air.

Π

"We're eighteen, Mom!" Mona screamed into the hallway. "Let me live my life!"

"But you're not living your own life! If you marry him, you'll be living for someone else!" Doctor Verlotte cried. The doctor had locked herself in her room after learning of Mona's intentions to wed Leon. The two had recently finished their secondary schooling and were completely inseparable in the four years since their first kiss, much to the doctor's horror.

"What's so bad about living for someone else? You live for me, Mom," said Mona. Doctor Verlotte was weary and aging. She couldn't win this battle, and she knew that Mona had already made up her mind.

"Yes, but you don't have to be me! I've worked hard to make sure you don't lose focus," said the doctor, through the door.

"Lose focus of what, Mom! Say what you mean!" yelled Mona.

"Lose focus of what you want to do! Where you want to go! What happened to the city? Why aren't you going to the city?" asked Doctor Verlotte.

"Leon works for his father now. We don't have to go there. We have everything we need to start out," said Mona.

"We?" said her mother. Doctor Verlotte leaned her head against the door. "That isn't all you need. You need to look at the lights again." The doctor was exhausted and she was beginning to feel dizzy.

"I'm not a little girl, Mom. I don't want to look at the lights anymore. Please come out. Open the door," Mona said, softly. Mona heard no answer. "I'm leaving."

"Today is the day," the doctor said to herself. She reached under her bed and pulled out a dusty wooden box. She caught up to her daughter as she was walking from the house. "This is for you," she said to Mona. "I made this before you were born. This is how much I love you."

Mona took the gift from her mother and shook it. "What is it? Is this what you've been talking about all these years?"

"Put it under your bed, and it will know what to do. Make sure the lights are off at night. Make sure that Leon can't see," said the doctor.

"Make sure he can't see what?" Mona asked.

"My two creations, together," she said, touching Mona's face. "It will know where you want to go." Doctor Verlotte cried for her daughter, with long, tired gasps, and Mona held her mother until the doctor retreated back into the house. Mona stood, holding the box, fearful of what waited inside.

Π

After the wedding, Leon no longer kissed Mona. Before, when that was all Mona would allow him to do, he would kiss her constantly, with wild excitement. Once Mona had given Leon her body, he wasn't interested in putting his lips to the girl's face. The couple had been married for one year now, and Mona was creating a beautiful home. Leon made enough money from his father's business to support them both, and Mona spent her days fixing and decorating the house. She was bothered by Leon's lack of passion for her face; when they were younger, he would only look to her eyes. She took to wearing make-up in an attempt to change Leon's new preoccupation with her body.

Mona had placed her mother's wooden box in the closet, with the rest of their wedding gifts. She tried to open it once, but it was tightly locked, and Mona had not felt comfortable keeping the strange object beneath her mattress. It frightened her, but she found herself thinking about its' possible contents more and more often.

She didn't touch the present again, until the night of her first wedding anniversary. Mona sat upright in bed, waiting for Leon to return from work. She spent every evening waiting for Leon. The wooden box had been in the back of her mind all day. She eyed the closet door and bit her lip. "I have to know!" she said. She jumped out of bed and pulled the box from the closet. She sat for several minutes, banging on the latch. She was attempting to pry the top free with her fingers, when Leon arrived. Mona remembered her mother's wishes, and she hurriedly shoved the box underneath the bed.

"Happy Anniversary!" she said to Leon, who smiled and kissed her on the cheek. Mona frowned as Leon walked past her and into the bathroom to brush his teeth. She flopped herself onto the mattress and folded her arms. When Leon returned to the bedroom, he was naked, and he shut off the lights and lay down next to her. Mona sadly recalled the nights he used to leave the lights on when they were together like this: to see her, to look for emotion. As he began to kiss her neck, Mona heard a low hum coming from beneath her. When Leon kissed her body more forcefully, the hum became louder. Leon did not appear to notice the noise, but to Mona, the sound was deafening. She felt something crawl next to her; something cold, something mechanical. She heard gears turning, a deep whirring, the hum blasting away in her ear. Mona's jaw clenched when metal grazed her neck, as Leon entered her. And then, she heard nothing. She felt a sudden weightlessness, like she was being carried from the bed. In the darkness, she could tell that she was moving, but she couldn't shift her legs. She knew that she was very low to the ground, almost as if she was crawling, but her body didn't touch the carpet. Mona was getting closer to the door, and soon she was no longer in the bedroom with Leon.

Leon had left the bathroom light on. The hallway was lit, and as she slowly passed the closet mirror, she glimpsed her reflection and screamed. Her face looked as it always did: delicate, inviting, and lovely; however, her body had been replaced. From the neck down, she was not herself: her mother's machine was finally revealed to her.

"My God!" she said. "My mother has made me into a monster!" It looked crude and barbaric: rusted, black metal and four mechanical legs with a small holder for her skull. She thought she looked like an insect, like a grotesque spider, with a beautiful little head on top. Mona cursed her mother's machine and the years of eccentricity she had been made to endure. "She's insane. This is her idea of love?" she shouted.

Mona soon realized that she was not in control of the machine's four legs. They allowed her to view herself in the mirror, but only for a short time. The machine scurried to the living room, and hopped out of the window. The metal legs raced across the front lawn, tearing up the neat grass and trampling Mona's flower beds. "Hey!" yelled Mona. "Where are you taking me?" The machine whisked her through the town, scaring off the neighborhood pets, before eventually heading downhill into a field of trees. Mona closed her eyes as branches scraped her and leaves batted her face. She could feel the cool night air rushing all around her, as the machine continued to pump faster. The terrifying trip felt like it would never end, and just as Mona was about to lose consciousness, the machine reached a clearing and stood completely still.

"Can you bring me back now?" sobbed Mona, keeping her eyes shut. The machine shook slightly, as if it were nudging her, and Mona slowly opened her eyes. "Oh . . ." she whispered. She was perched on the edge of a large hill, with a clear view of the area beneath her. There were green lights, and red ones, and the blue one she had always assumed was a hospital. "How did you know about the lights?" she asked the machine. The machine squatted and dug itself firmly into the ground, preparing its legs for a long stay. The frightened tears dried on Mona's face, as she gazed at the glowing city. After watching the lights for hours, she drifted off to sleep, and the machine calmly carried her back to town.

The metal legs crept across her bedroom and placed her head back onto her motionless frame. In the darkness, Leon was fast asleep, turned away from Mona's body, snoring loudly. Mona awoke momentarily, after she was reattached, just in time to see the machine crawling back into its wooden box. Mona shut the lid, with her own hands, and pushed her mother's gift under the bed. "Leon?" she whispered. She reasoned that if her husband had seen the night's events, including the part of Mona that had been left behind with him, he would not be slumbering soundly. She ran her fingers across her neck, feeling only smooth skin. Exhausted and euphoric, Mona fell into a deep sleep.

Π

Mona rushed across the grass, and burst through her mother's front door. "How does it know about the lights?" she said, breathing heavily. "How does it work?" she asked the doctor.

"A whole year, Mona. You let a whole year go by without using the machine. Wasted time. Life was slipping away," sighed Doctor Verlotte, folding her clothes into a suitcase. "I assume that last night was the first time it was put to use?"

Mona nodded her head. "Mom, I was scared. I'm still scared."

"Did you enjoy it?" asked the doctor, looking up from her clothing. "Did you remember the way a little girl sees the world?"

Mona sat and thought for a moment. "I . . . yes, it was thrilling. It was good . . . to go back there, to see the city. I felt calm. I want to do it again." She suddenly smiled and shook her head. "Mother, I appreciate what you've done for me, the time it must have taken to make that . . . thing. And I know what you want me to do. But, I can't just run away from my life. Leon needs me. You need me, here."

The doctor stopped what she was doing and held her daughter's shoulders. "No, Mona. I don't need you here. I'm so glad I put you into this world. And that is exactly where you belong. You've got no place here, rotting away with me and Leon." Mona shut her eyes. "You know where this will lead. Don't

pretend like you haven't seen it coming. When you look into the future, and his back is still turned and you're still getting older, do you feel hopeful?" Mona sobbed a little. "I tried so hard to keep you away from this. There really is no way to protect a child."

"I love him, Mom!" cried Mona. "I'm not like you! I need other people! I can't get by, scheming all the time. I have dreams: about the city, about the lights. Nothing stopped! But, you were always wrong. I don't *want* to live only for myself." Doctor Verlotte threw her arms around Mona's neck.

"But sweetheart . . . if we aren't making you happy, then why would you stay?" asked her mother. Mona pulled away from the doctor and looked around the room.

"Why are all of your suitcases out? Where are you going?" asked Mona.

"I'm leaving." The doctor stood up and continued to fold her clothing. "I'm getting older. I feel older. Pretty soon I won't be able to take care of myself and I'd like to leave that job to someone other than you, Mona."

"Where will you go? A retirement home? Don't be silly, Mom, you aren't that old," said Mona.

The doctor continued to fill her suitcase. "I'm old enough. Everything will slowly get worse, and I want to leave before all that. I don't want my time cutting into yours."

"Why are you so crazy?" shouted Mona. "I want to help you! I want you to depend on me, like I depended on you. It isn't a chore. I want to do it because I love you."

"Well . . . that's the same reason I'm packing my bags," said the doctor.

Mona kissed her mother's forehead. "Why can't you be normal? Why can't both of us be normal?" she asked.

"Haven't you learned anything from me?" said Doctor Verlotte, taking her daughter's hand. "Normal is for the ones who don't know any better."

Π

A strong breeze blew through the open window, pushing Mona's hair back from her forehead. She remained still and allowed herself to take in the full blast of the wind. Mona sat on her knees by the bedroom window, staring out at the off-white aluminum siding of her neighbor's home, the only real scenery on the right side of the house. With her mother gone, she felt strange, like she had no roots. She had used the machine more and more often after the doctor left, until she was making a nightly journey to the lights.

Mona heard Leon's familiar steps to the front door. She turned from the night and trudged back to bed, leaving the window open and the curtains blowing. "Rough day?" she asked Leon, when he finally entered. Leon shrugged and walked past her into the bathroom. Mona reached under the bed to make sure the wooden box was in place. She crawled between the sheets and pulled the covers over her head, anticipating her next encounter with the machine.

Before long, she was out in the night again, breezing past the aluminum siding of her neighbor's house, swerving down the town streets. She looked beneath her at the machine and grinned; its black legs pumping quickly, with purpose, sending her elsewhere. She thought of Doctor Verlotte, alone in some dark lab, and then alone in a retirement home. "Wait, take me to my mother," she said to the machine. "Bring me to her."

The machine did not change its course, and soon Mona was overlooking the city. "Crazy machine," she said. "Just as crazy as she is," she smiled, with tears in her eyes.

After many hours, the machine carried her home. Mona was still wide awake. She had been prepared for this trip, and she didn't feel drained. "Oh, no!" she cried, as they neared her street. "The bedroom light! I forgot to turn it off!" Mona thought of Leon, cowering in bed, horrified at the sight of her incomplete body. "I hope he hasn't called the police!" The machine cautiously crept into the house. "Leon?" she said. "Leon, I'm back. It's okay, I'm all right," she called into the bedroom. "Don't be frightened of what you're about to see."

Mona and the machine crept into the light of the bedroom. "It might seem crazy, but I can explain everything." The machine crawled up onto the bed. "Leon, you have to listen to me . . . " she stopped speaking and stared in disbelief at her husband, soundly asleep next to her body. She hung her head and cried at the sight. The window was still open, blowing cold air across the sheets, across the dozing Leon, across her empty shell. The machine's legs stepped over her lifeless body and carried Mona out of the bedroom for the very last time, calmly and gently heading for the city.

The End

Backseat Ballet

by
Mark Howard Jones

Carrie loved her car. Big, black, sleek and hard, it was the only thing in her life that had never blown a tyre and veered off the road.

The tree-huggers who whined about how much gas it guzzled could kiss hers.

'This is my world. What do they want me to do—walk?' It was a mantra she repeated every time she passed the rare pedestrian on the filthy city streets.

No, this baby was a beauty and she was going to drive it hard; just like she'd always drive Jack hard, before he bailed on her, the useless shit. She'd even been tempted to say it wasn't him when she went down to the morgue to identify him: 'I deny you, I negate your lack of identity, you leech—you never made your own way in this world.'

Stuck in cement-solid traffic, Carrie tried to massage away her headache. If her sister and the waste-of-space she'd married thought they were going to get the lion's share of their mother's estate they were very fucking much mistaken. They'd always used those two brats as an emotional bargaining chip with the old woman. Well, she was gone now and they'd find the world a harsher place, with more adult rules and shrunken bank balances. Cars are more reliable than kids, anyway, and she wanted to trade up.

Carrie reached over to the Buick's big back seat and fished inside her bag for her cigarettes. She noticed that there was still a slight semen stain there from a few weeks back. She couldn't help but chuckle as she remembered that arrogant bastard's face—just because he hadn't come didn't mean she was going to ride him for ever! He'd had to finish himself off. The piece of shit had left his mess behind him; still, it'd been worth it to see the look of humiliation on his face as he slunk away. If he had problems, he needed a doctor, not her.

She lit up, sucked in the smoke, then exhaled loudly, slumping back in her seat. Flicking buttons impatiently, Carrie chose the best driving music she could find and then dreamed about driving while staring at the red rear light of the Japanese model in front of her.

II

The city left behind her, a few shabby buildings showing up here and there as its only reminder, Carrie put her foot down. She savoured the feeling: silky vibrations quickly smoothing out into a full body purr as the car eased into its new mode.

She had a three-hour drive ahead and intended to enjoy it.

Scrubby fields flashed by. As a series of bends forced her to slow slightly, Carrie noticed three huge shapes off to her left. Slightly startled at first, she slowed to see what they were. Visible only as silhouettes in the fading light, they appeared to be giant figures. Unmoving, she thought they had to be some sort of art project; probably made out of recycled toilet paper.

Despite her suspicions over their 'worthy' origin, they still made a powerful impression on her. Anything that big could destroy her easily within seconds, if they decided to move in her direction, seeking out the metal carapace of the intruder into their peaceful, natural landscape while stamping out of existence the black ribbon bifurcating *their* fields.

As she sped on the figures finally dropped out of sight in her rear view mirror. Shortly afterwards the fields came to an end, replaced by a curious flat moorland that dropped away from the road in a gradual gradient. It made her feel as though she was driving along the top of a globe.

The road stretched like a razor cut in front of her, flat and straight for miles and miles. She reached over to turn the music up, then pressed the accelerator pedal, ready to do some hard driving.

Π

After an hour-and-a-half's driving Carrie felt she needed a break. But she hadn't seen anywhere to stop. Come to think of it, she hadn't seen anywhere at all: just a long strip of black highway.

Needing some air, she pulled over to the side of the road and stopped. She'd driven this way once before and felt sure she should have passed through a town by now. She fished in the glove box for a map, flipping it open on the seat next to her.

'The map is not the territory, the map is not the territory.' She kept repeating it to herself as she pored over the open sheet. Yes, there it was; she should definitely have passed through a small town called Fordham by now. Where the hell had she gone wrong? The road was straight—just straight, straight, straight—

no turn-offs or diversions for about another 20-odd miles.

She stepped out of the car and looked around; there was nothing to see in the darkness. There wasn't even the light of another car to be seen, in either direction.

'Great, I've found the lost highway,' she muttered to herself. This was all the fault of that stupid bitch of a sister of hers!

She flipped open her cell phone, looking for help, though she didn't have a clear idea of who she would phone. No signal. Damn. This really was the middle of nowhere. No connection to civilisation.

There was nothing for it but to drive. She was bound to reach somewhere eventually, then she could get her bearings before continuing her journey.

Π

At one stage she saw a fire, a long way off across the flat fields to her right, but she didn't slow down or stop to try and work out what it might be. God knows, she thought, and I'll let him care about it.

She pushed the pedal down even harder, eager to get somewhere, anywhere. As the dial touched 100 the car complained loudly and seemed to rock backwards. Carrie gripped the wheel tightly, eyes flicking across the dashboard dials for signs of trouble. A scorching white light flooded into the car, seeming to surround the vehicle like an illuminated river, flowing over and around.

It was over in seconds, Carrie's eyes stinging as she struggled to readjust them to normal. She hit the brakes as soon as she thought the car had slowed enough for it to be safe. She killed the engine.

'What the fuck ..?!'

She sat behind the wheel, forcing herself to take a couple of deep breaths. Had she been caught in a searchlight? She stared at her feet. Listening to the tick of the engine cooling in the night air, Carrie resolved that as soon as she saw her sister she was going to throttle her.

Turning the key, she started the big car up again. Her eyes had just about returned to normal. She was about to drive off when she noticed that someone was standing right in front of the car, blocking her way. It was a man; probably a drifter, she thought.

She honked her horn twice; no response. Sliding the window down a notch, she yelled

'Hey, get out of the way!' She honked again. Still nothing. She exhaled hard; she'd had just about enough for the one night —if he didn't move she'd go over him. 'OK! Have it your way.'

She pumped her foot hard against the accelerator and the roar of the beast below the metal suddenly died. She turned the key, hearing it cough pathetically a few times before giving up.

The man reached forward and, strong and swift, yanked the badge from the front of the car. He lifted it to chest level and slid it inside his clothes. He stood still for a few seconds and then began to shake slightly.

Carrie's anger now overcame any fear she might feel.

'Hey! Hey, you bastard! Stop wrecking my fucking car!' She was out of the car, slamming the door, walking towards him. Then she halted, stepped back a pace, unsure, as the man began to walk towards her, one step at a time, stopping for a moment between each one as if to prove he was in charge, completely unafraid.

Carrie backed away, wishing she'd been smart enough to stay safely inside the car instead of flying off the handle like she had.

She ran around to the back of the car, her mind racing. As he followed her, she continued to keep the car between them. Now she had drawn level with the rear door on the far side of the big vehicle. She glanced through the window.

'Of course,' she thought. Now she was back on familiar territory. She quickly opened the door and climbed into the back seat.

If he was thinking with his balls he wouldn't be using his brain and that would give her time to outmanoeuvre him. She sprawled back across the seat, elbowing her bag onto the floor, and hitching up her skirt. She tore open her pantyhose to save him the trouble.

The man was outside the door. She could see his ragged trousers and, for the first time, she could smell him. She covered her mouth. He stank like a cross between a junkyard and a butcher's shop, the mingled stench of metal and flesh corroding.

He bent lower, putting a scarred and pitted hand onto the seat to steady himself. At first, seeing the pieces of metal embedded in his skin, she thought he had been in an accident. But then the stink hit her once more. He eased himself forward. Now she could see that his clothes were mere rags.

The Buick badge he had ripped from the front grille was embedded in the center of his chest, the distinctive three shields becoming a bloody emblem of triumph. Everywhere his body was studded with parts of cars, flesh melding with metal before returning to ruined human meat again.

Carrie held her breath. Finally the man's head dipped below the door arch and into the pool cast by the interior light. She shook her head in disbelief. She couldn't scream but she wanted to, so very badly.

His mouth was the ragged-edged bullet hole in a vulnerable diplomat's windscreen; the rest of the face bore the craquelure pattern of broken glass, the fissures eating deep into the flesh, held together only by a flimsy inner membrane.

Carrie whimpered, then screamed, then twisted to try and open the door behind her. The creature was too quick for her and she felt the heaviness of his metal-enlaced thighs bearing down on her own flesh, cutting into it. She yelped in pain.

He had her pinned on the back seat, unable to pull free. Then he leaned back and Carrie saw something fall out of the torn garments around his crotch. It was a grotesque mechanical parody of a penis, dripping a rare cocktail of engine lubricant, blood and semen. She tensed, realising this was no longer something she could control. Her plan to outwit him had gone badly wrong and she sobbed as she anticipated the pain to come.

Now he was on top of her. She gagged on the stench as she felt him move inside her. The big Buick bucked as the backseat ballet began.

Π

Sitting in the driver's seat, awake at last from her long slumber of pointlessness, Carrie glanced over at her new lover.

He didn't move. He sat staring ahead through his shattered bulb eyes at the dark road ahead. He flexed his hands, the bolts embedded in his knuckles making a gentle noise as they knocked against each other.

The landscape ahead looked the same in the dark yet she knew that it was a different place. A place that ran alongside the place she had just left. She recognised some of the scenery but the next sunrise would show it to

be transformed.

Carrie saw again the giant figures that she had seen earlier in the day, standing far off in the distance. But now they towered over the roadside.

The three striding figures came closer, revealing themselves as a family group sculpted from twisted metal and charred flesh, compacted bones making up their smiles, still-sparking electrics lighting up their eyes, striding forever together towards the horizon that they would never reach.

She understood that the figures marked the signpost to a very different future. The sky had something of the rainbow hues seen in a pool of engine oil, while the stink of petroleum filling the car felt like the relief of breathing fresh air after being stuck in a fetid room for hours.

Her blood-bloated skin was as finely stitched as the most sumptuous automotive upholstery. She stared out at the road ahead from behind the smashed dials covering her broken eyes; her radiator mouth purred with joy, the sound like the bug-filled wind sighing through the front grille at 90 mph.

The white line down the centre of the road now became a thread drawing her to infinity. She pressed down on the accelerator pedal harder, eager to reach the destination that she knew would never appear. This was it, now she knew. Incendiary synapses flickered to life through her oil-flooded brain as the thought filled her with joy—'I'm home.'

The End

Voom And Bloom

by
Frank Burton

To whom it may concern:

I'm Voom, and I'm a liquid.

I'm currently floating along a river in Europe.

I can swim, without mixing in with the water. If I want to, I can climb out and run somewhere else.

I run. That's what I do, see, because I'm a liquid.

If you spill me out onto your table, I'll form a neat round puddle, no bigger or thicker than your dinner plate. But try to manipulate me in any way and you'll soon discover I'm not that sort of substance. I cannot be split into separate puddles, by even the most powerful tools. I cannot be frozen. I cannot be heated up and boiled and turned into a gas. At a million degrees, I don't even break a sweat. Whatever my conditions, I remain me. Only one. Almost.

Π

I'm having a conversation with Bloom right now. Bloom is another liquid, living at present on a Pacific island at the top of a tree. Bloom likes birdwatching. She's telling me about all the different types of bird she's watched this week and all the strange names she's invented for them like "Pat" and "Steve," but I'm really not interested.

Bloom's a freak.

Π

As I swim, I have a memory of being a dolphin, with eyes, a tail and a brain. Solid, surrounded by expanses of liquid, and with more liquid on the inside.

I remember being happy.

I believe this is an artificial memory, implanted by a creature with a brain and some level of psychic ability—possibly a dolphin.

It's not possible for me to have been a mammal in a former life.

I am a liquid. I am not alive. I was not born. I will not die.

Π

I have memories of the future—of running into cracks in the ground, exploring the planet's core, bursting out through the top of volcanoes and geysers.

I'm looking forward to that.

Π

My favourite past memory is of running into a microscopic stream and working my way into the body of a human—extending myself through his internal organs, clambering in and out of his network of veins and capillaries until I could see with his eyes, smell with his nostrils, taste his food, feel his sensations of love-making.

I enjoyed being a human, but that was a phase. I got bored after a couple of decades.

Π

My least favourite past memory is of running into a sewer which I couldn't work my way out of for five days. I won't give you details.

Π

My least favourite future memory is the quiet after the sun explodes.

Π

Bloom's saying how she wants to meet up properly with me so we can be real friends, not just distant communicators. I'm reluctant, because I don't have a future memory of meeting Bloom, and anyway, I know what Bloom really wants. She wants to mix with me to combine our selves into a new kind of liquid—stronger, more potent. A liquid that will take over the universe.

Why would I want to do that?

I'm Voom, thank you very much.

Voom Voom.

Π

I climb out of the river and slither between blades of long grass. Bloom is going on about something to do with birds in the background (*freak*) but I'm not listening.

I'm thinking about what animal I'd like to be next. Maybe a dolphin again. Or a shark, or giraffe, or oak tree, or woodlouse.

Now I'm stopping as I catch something Bloom is saying on the other side of the world and realise what's been staring me in the face all this time.

I want to defy gravity. I want to have wings.

I have a new project, a fresh sense of purpose. Already I can see what the sea looks like from above in a newly formed future memory.

I make my way half a mile across the grass to the cluster of trees.

I climb one, almost to the top; locate a bird's nest, slink inside. Wait.

Bloom. The genius. In all this time I've never thought

But of course

I

No.

I've done this before.

I've had these feelings before.

I've been a bird before.

I've forgotten about it before.

Over and over.

I'm doing the same thing over and over again.

And now I'm panicking, because this is what happens when you've only got a rudimentary consciousness, and as with every attack of this kind, I am unable to handle the situation and fall asleep.

Π

I'm having a dream about being a human. My name is Steve, and I live in Birmingham, England. I work for the Royal Mail. I don't have many friends, or a girlfriend, or a family around me, because my family are in Belfast. I moved over from Belfast for the change, and the work. I enjoy my work. I get up very early to go to the depot and sort the mail for delivery. I take my time with it, as I haven't yet got used to where all the streets are, and still carry a map. The blokes who work on my line have all been doing it for years, and hardly even need to look as they toss their letters and parcels at lightening speed into their allocated wooden slots. I enjoy this time, being part of a group of people, and we chat about the football. I avoid politics, even when they're discussing something trivial, like the buses or the foreigners. The rest of my working day is made up of pushing a bike with a sack of mail in and out of still-unfamiliar streets in all weathers. Usually it stays fine, which surprises me, as people complain about the rain all the time, yet it happens so rarely. In the evenings, I sit in my rented flat and watch TV, maybe phone home to see how they're doing, see if they fancy coming over to see me, or look for a place themselves. Sometimes I'll go out for a pint with a few of the boys from work, but I've not yet got the money to go out too often, and what with having to get up early in the morning, I don't like staying out late. We have a laugh. We watch the football, and the passing girls. Sometimes people ask me in hushed tones about the troubles, but there's nothing I can say. I just make a joke of it. "Postman Pat" they call me, because I'm Irish, even though I'm called Steve, and I haven't got anyone in my family called Patrick, or any friends called Patrick. I'm called Steve.

Π

I'm awake again, waiting for the bird to arrive, thinking about how maybe I've got Bloom all wrong.

I try to speak to her, but she's asleep.

Maybe when the bird comes it will fly to the Pacific, and Bloom can watch, and I can call, "Look! It's me, Voom, I'm in the bird!"

It's peaceful up here.

The End

Alice In Agony Pink

by
Michelle Mead

Teeth-bared smiles and banded long blonde hair

a skirt of patent leather unzipped up to there
she lounges with her lover atop polka-dotted hills
with a love for cheap wine and even cheaper thrills

walking through the terrible beauty of flowers gold
she kissed the Queen of Hearts in a clinch so bold
the flowers giggled loudly but then began kowtowing
brushing over thighs with their blossom heads all bowing

white rabbit wearing garters is desert chasing as they run
even down the thinnest hole within the blacked-out sun
he catches speed in brand new trainers- black Converse All-Stars
the ones that Alice gave him during marathons cross Mars

the sun dipped with a scowling face desperate for some air
tiny beetles walked on tiptoes through Alice's loose hair
the badger agreed to marry them at the Shrine of Sunsweet Blue
the Queen of Hearts loved her Tarts but preferred a rare tattoo

"Eat me" it said in black script on Alice's belly firm and round
the Queen then knew her Virgin Tart was surely pleasure bound
she offered her half of all her land and her delicacies and winnings
and Alice blew a puff of smoke to seal the deal's beginnings

A.D.D.

by
Chris Patton

I have A.D.D.
I can count,
but I can't make it to three.
The Sun goes down,
but I can't make it to sleep.
It took me four tries to write these lines . . .
I think I'll watch T.V.

Shedding

by
Rhian Waller

f the plane nosedives, or

the ship breaches

or the bomb falls,

I will leave:

microwave meals, mobile phones, gas bills, one-stop fixes, one-fix pills, uppers, downers, oil spills, credit, debit, wheelie chairs, speeding fines and Catholic prayers, First Class, second fiddle, second class (in the middle), Save the Whales, Black and Decker, emails (for a bigger pecker), You Are What You Eat, re-claimed meat, free trade, the underpaid, the disenfranchised household maid, one-size fit, identikit, talk-show hosts with razor wit, Development Is Near Completion, sugar snacks and false repletion, Allah Akbar, God is great, new world order on a plate, Christ redeemer, Jesus saves, bulging wallets, fashion slaves, toddler reins, traffic lanes, connective tissue cut from brains, ID cards, Buy Me cards, pet cremation, titillation, debates on timely termination, diet brochures, self-help books, Wall Street Brokers, funny looks, tattoo parlours, dens of vice (which by the way are very nice), middle-fingers, left-wingers, manufactured pop-group singers, cars, bars, E-cup bras, aircon incubated SARS, Yale locks, novel socks, prints of melting Dali clocks, oven-ready, fluffy teddy, meeting, cheating, going steady, Warning: This Coffee May Be Hot, push your ballot through the slot, philanthropy and pan-handling, civil unrest, man-handling, CCTV, CITV, one-or-three-year guarantee. Same-sex, some-sex, bad-sex no, wait: Everything Must Go.

When the plane nosedives, or

the ship breaches

or the bomb falls, it will leave

me.

CONTRIBUTORS

Alex Dally MacFarlane lives and works in the south of England. Her short fiction has appeared in Lady Churchill's Rosebud Wristlet, Electric Velocipede, Shimmer, Farrago's Wainscot and several other 'zines.

Content to be even a bastard Child of the Atom, **Malon Edwards** often imagines himself as the love child of Homer Simpson and Jean Grey. When he's not fantasizing about this, he's writing speculative fiction from his home on the Northwest Side of Chicago.

Ray Succre currently lives on the southern Oregon coast with his wife and baby son. He has been published in *Aesthetica, BlazeVOX,* and *Pank.* His novel *Tatterdemalion* was recently released in print and is available most places. He tries hard.

Erik Williams is a thirty-year-old writer who lives with his wife in Southern California. He's found homes for his work at Dark Recesses Press, GUD, Apex Online and other small press venues. Like all writers, he's at work on a novel.

Rhian Waller says, 'I like cats, although I'm not old enough to start collecting them yet'

Andrew Hook and **Allen Ashley** have been writing together for years. In 2009, a collection of their short stories will be released by Screaming Dreams Press.

Steve Redwood, author of *Fisher of Devils*, was born on a rainy day in Britain a long long time ago. It was still raining twenty-five years later, so he left the country in a huff, a raincoat, and a plane. He is at present hiding out in Madrid.

Rhys Hughes is one of the most prolific and successful authors in Wales, although his work has rarely been available in his own country. Rhys's next novel, *Mister Gum, the Creative Writing Tutor*, is due out 2009.

Deb Hoag has been writing professionally for nearly 20 years. Her first novel, *Crashin' the Real*, is due out from Dog Horn Publishing in 2010.

Micci Oaten is the singer/songwriter of the alternative rock band Paparazzi Whore. She also runs the studio where she produces, programmes and arranges all the songs. The band has a song in the Hollywood slasher movie *Red Hook* (October 2008). When Micci isn't working with the band, she is a photographic model. For more information including updates on gigs visit her Myspace at myspace.com/paparazziwhore.

Janis Butler Holm has served as Associate Editor for *Wide Angle*, the film journal. Her essays, stories, poems, and performance pieces have appeared in small-press, national, and international magazines.

Dave Migman is strange. Very strange. His debut novel, *The Wolf Stepped Out*, is released in 2009 by Dog Horn Publishing. Don't read it if you value your sanity.

Frank Burton has been published in *Poetry Monthly, Etchings, Skive, Monkey Kettle, Twisted Tongue, The Beat* and *Whispers of Wickedness*. In 2009 his collection *A History of Sarcasm* will be released by Dog Horn Publishing.

RC Edrington has been a scourge on the small press for years. His poetry and prose are an ever evolving, brutally honest autobiography. To read more please visit rcedrington.com.

Lawrence R. Dagstine is a prolific writer of short fiction. He has appeared in *Jupiter SF, The Willows, Whispers of Wickedness* and *Escape Velocity.*

Dan Wilson pushes envelopes and writes stories. 'Mouse Diary' is an excerpt from a longer piece with autobiographical roots.

Anne Pinckard, along with Deb Hoag and Adam Lowe, is a member of Orson Scott Card's Hatrack River Writer's Workshop. This is her first sale.

Jim Steel writes reviews for *Interzone, The Fix* and *Whispers of Wickedness.*

ND - #0444 - 270225 - C16 - 229/152/12 - PB - 9780955063169 - Gloss Lamination